OF
PIXIES
AND
PROMISES

OF
PIXIES
AND
PROMISES

LANA
PECHERCZYK

BLURB

As a lethal Reaper, Sid kills monstrous fae. He's spent his life blocking the little voice in his head saying his loyalties are misplaced. But humans can't be wrong. It's the fae who hoard the earth's bounty and banish humanity to live behind cold gray walls. But when a lone, captivating pixie dares to face his soldiers pillaging her forest, he knows his priorities are about to shift.

On the eve of her coronation, Princess Nyra feels less than worthy when her wings refuse to make pixie dust. Without it, she can't choose a consort, let alone receive the power required to keep her gully safe. When she stumbles across humans illegally mining her precious forest, she wants to prove she's still worthy of protecting her people... with or without a consort.

But her sabotage backfires, and her handsome enemy unexpectedly saves her life. Suddenly shrunk to bug size and without magic, they're forced to trust each other to survive the perilous journey home. With each step, their forbidden attraction grows. But when one is lying and a promise is broken, the gully won't be the only thing in danger of becoming a wasteland. Nyra's heart will never flourish again.

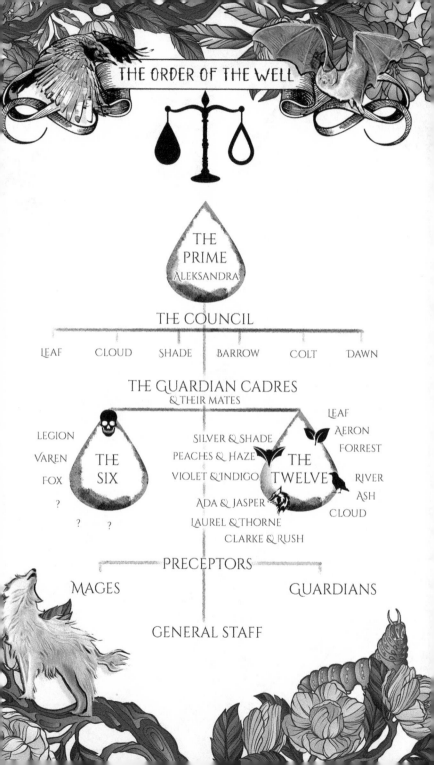

THE ORDER OF THE WELL

THE PRIME
ALEKSANDRA

THE COUNCIL

| LEAF | CLOUD | SHADE | BARROW | COLT | DAWN |

THE GUARDIAN CADRES
& THEIR MATES

LEGION
VAREN
FOX
?
? ?

THE SIX

LEAF
AERON
FORREST

SILVER & SHADE
PEACHES & HAZE
VIOLET & INDIGO
ADA & JASPER
LAUREL & THORNE
CLARKE & RUSH

THE TWELVE

RIVER
ASH
CLOUD

PRECEPTORS

MAGES   GUARDIANS

GENERAL STAFF

EL

WINTER COURT
ACONITE CITY

ACONITE SEA

ICE WITCH

THE ICE FOREST

HUMAN TERRITORY

UNSEELIE KINGDOM

SEELIE KINGDOM

CRYSTAL
CITY

RUSH'S
CABIN

MEANDER
WOOD

WHISPERING
WOODS

CRESCENT
HOLLOW

FOREWORD

This novella was originally published in the Babe
Anthology in 2023. It has been revised and updated here.
Enjoy your trip to Elphyne.

"If you don't pick your dicks soon, they'll be picked for you."

Nyra ignored the unsolicited advice from her mother's sister, Colt. Colt was a good friend and a Mage at the Order of the Well. She wasn't required to have a harem. She didn't understand.

As a trusted Councillor at the Order, Colt had a purpose. She had a life. She was only here to help with the coronation ball. Soon she would return to overseeing magic use in Elphyne, and Nyra would be left struggling to fit into this tribe alone.

After turning four and thirty this spring, Nyra's wings still hadn't created pixie dust. But it wasn't as though she could control it. The wings dusted who they wanted. The Well had plans, and maybe having a harem—or any mate—wasn't in Nyra's future. The sooner everyone accepted it, the better.

Instead of wallowing, Nyra focused on finger painting bioluminescent art on the tree hollow walls in preparation for her coronation. Pixies bustled about behind them, decorating the vast space and trying not to eavesdrop, but Nyra was done suffering in silence. As far as she was concerned, having a harem had nothing to do with her ability to rule. It might affect how much magic she could draw from the Well or how big their tribe might be, but they wouldn't know until she was coronated.

"Nyra," Colt said. "Are you listening?"

"I'm listening," she replied in a sing-song voice and scribbled a mustache onto the character painted on the wall... who just happened to have the same rainbow wings, hair, and dusky brown skin as Colt.

Colt's wings vibrated in vexation. Wind and dust stirred, ruining the wet paint of Nyra's work. She scowled and faced her aunt.

"Was that necessary?" Colt's eyebrow arched as she took in the mustache with a pout. The expression flared the glowing blue teardrop mark on her bottom lip—her Mage mark. It was a reminder that Colt was respected in the broader community, and Nyra was still a recalcitrant youth. "You could have at least painted one on your mother. It's not my fault you're in this predicament."

Bitterness seethed in Nyra's stomach. Colt had no clue what Nyra went through. *No clue.*

Queen Juniper's figure was painted next to Nyra's. Her age was determined not by wrinkles on her skin but by the luminosity of her wings. They were dull, unlike Nyra's prismatic, sparkling set. The queen had the same pastel pink hair and golden skin, but Nyra's hair floated around her face in wisps that tickled her shoulders. It was tied in a fancy woven design to prepare for the ball, but strands kept falling out. The queen's tresses flowed in waves that gave vibrance where her wings failed. Her hair never looked messy like Nyra's.

But those dull wings were a glaring truth. The queen's magic was fading. It was time for her heir to accept the tithe from the Well in return for protecting their little pocket of Elphyne. This tithe was too powerful for one little pixie queen to contain and required the full capacity of a harem.

"What is necessary," Colt pressed. "Is that you remember your duty. Time is running out, and if we don't have a new queen to unite the power of this tribe, then we cannot fight threats to our peace. The Athyrium Gully Tribe, the largest pixie tribe in all of Elphyne, will be dissolved into your rivals. Is that the legacy you want?"

"Can't I just run away and join the Order like you?"

"As much as I'd like to have you with me, there are no other heirs. I was the spare. When you came along, I was free to do as I pleased. It is too late for me to return. As a Councillor, I have responsibilities to the entire land, not just this tribe."

Nyra groaned and rolled to her belly. She rubbed her finger through the bioluminescent algae on the clay ground. If only it were as simple as painting the glow back onto her mother's wings, she could remain queen for a little longer. Nyra wasn't done exploring and being young. Four and thirty was virtually a child in fae years. Her mother's life was three centuries long, and she would live longer still... just not as the active queen.

"Since your fathers died," Colt said, but Nyra bared her fangs and hissed a warning. She hated talking about their deaths. Unruffled, Colt continued. "There has been a gaping hole in the amount of mana your tribe collectively farms, and the gully needs to be nurtured."

"I know, I know." Nyra sniffed. It wasn't only her mother's wings that faded. The plants were dimming, and the animals in the gully were leaving for greener pastures. Soon the forest would look as gray as the desecrated dead lands around Crystal City. She shuddered at the thought. It all started with the attack that stole her fathers' lives. The three King Consorts in her mother's harem had died protecting Queen Juniper during a human-led raid less than a decade ago. Nyra felt the pain of that loss as acutely as if it happened today.

"Since the great freeze," Colt said, "and the ruin of the old world, the Well has entrusted the upkeep of nature to us woodland fae. The elves, the oak men, the stags, and pixies." Colt's wings dragged as she moved about the cave, pointing to the artwork they'd both painted over the week as part of Nyra's pre-coronation ritual. She stopped at a dark human city covered with icy ominous clouds. "Humanity had custody of this land for generations. But they destroyed it with their metals, plastics, and greedy wars." She moved to another picture—snowy landscapes and everything white and frozen. "The wasteland was barely survivable." She moved to a third image—blue, glowing water bubbling from the ice, leaving magical things in its wake. Green life. Fae. "And then the Well miraculously gave us a second chance. It connected us on a level unseen for eons. It is because we are connected to the land that we protect it. If we fail it now, we circle back to this."

Colt patted the dark, destructive cloud looming over the gray cities of the old world. Nyra shivered. A grey city already existed in this world. It grew cloudier and darker by the year. Crystal City was where humanity quarantined themselves and hid for centuries from their mistake, letting the fae do all the hard work of fostering this broken world back to life.

Nyra's upper lip curled with bitterness. Humans stole her fathers, and now they wanted to steal precious resources buried deep beneath the gully. *Well, they can't have it.* Whether or not Nyra found a harem, whether or not the Well accepted her as the new queen, she would give her dying breath to keep humans out of their territory.

She would find a way.

"Nrya—"

"Enough!" Nyra gnashed her fangs. Her wings fluttered and lifted her to a standing position. "I've heard enough, Colt. My duty to my people isn't the problem."

Pity entered Colt's eyes as she glanced at Nyra's wings. "Still haven't created pixie dust?"

Nyra's gaze dipped. "No."

"You need to give some dicks a chance. Dusting might occur on the outside, but it starts within."

Nyra's brow arched. "You think that's the problem? That I don't want it or haven't tried?"

Colt shrugged. "Is it?"

"I've danced in the sky with half the single males my age. Believe me. Wanting and trying is *not* the problem."

"The Well-blessed human Seelie High Queen is an incredible healer and mated to a shifter. Perhaps if you visit the Summer Palace with a gift, she might have an elixir or something to fix you."

Great. Now I'm defective.

"No," Nyra snapped. "If my wings aren't making dust, then none of these miscreants are my mates. That's all there is to it. And I'm not the type to wait for them to find me."

"Why not let me or your mother pick your consorts? Then you don't have to worry."

"I don't need you to pick my dicks." Nyra sighed. "I may never go into heat without pixie dust. Without an heir, what kind of queen am I?"

"What are you going to do?"

"Start protecting the gully on my own." Nyra's wings fluttered, and she walked to the cave exit.

"Wait, your dress!"

But she was done listening to all the reasons she was failing. She needed to get out of there.

Nyra stepped out of the tree hollow, her wings vibrated, and she became airborne and weightless. She shifted from dragonfly size to full-fae size in a blink, uncaring that she drained most of her internal well to do so. She still had enough *mana* to protect herself should she need it.

Colt didn't follow, which meant she either had no mana left to grow in size or had decided it wasn't worth another argument.

Good.

Nyra needed to be alone.

She flew through the ferns and lush green underbrush, then up as she twined around the tall trees. Her flowing ballgown caught on a branch. Nyra heard a distinct rip and winced but kept flying until she burst through the canopy into sun-warmed air. She inhaled deeply and faced the bright orb. A flock of parrots flew by as she basked, pelting her rudely.

She hissed and snapped her fangs. If she were small, she'd have spiraled and potentially lost equilibrium. But she grinned as she caught them flying in formation. It looked wonderful. Freeing.

And exactly what she needed. Throwing caution to the wind, she joined them—shrinking back into dragonfly size so she could coast in their slipstream and forget about the world. Whoops—*there went another chunk of her mana stores.* But there was no substitution for the wind beneath her wings and her troubles behind her.

A curl of smoke wafted from the forest nearby. Peeling away from the flock, she spread her wings and corkscrewed down to survey the land as she dropped.

That smoke was too thick for hunters—both human or fae. Was it a catastrophe? A wildfire? She concentrated on her connection to the gully and immediately felt something was wrong but couldn't understand why.

She buzzed closer, coasted, buzzed forward, then a horrendous crash vibrated through the gully. She startled. Trees screamed as they were cut viciously from their root systems. Someone was logging. No, it was worse than logging—they were reaping. Raiding.

"*Humans,*" she hissed.

It must be. Fae would work harmoniously with the trees. Elves magically grew plants for furniture and buildings to not hurt the forest. That scream—it could also be Oak Men. They sometimes looked so similar to the trees that it was hard to tell them apart. A human would have no clue.

Keeping her small shape to avoid detection, Nyra flew closer to the disruption. It definitely wasn't loggers—although they'd cut down a few trees to make space. The sound came from a metal machine on wheels. It had a manticore's tail that reached over its head and dug into the ground, tearing it up to expose what lay beneath.

Digging?

Taking?

That was the source of the most pain. A group of humans stood around the hole. Some worked on unearthing while others stood guard. Some cut wood from the tree they'd felled and piled the offcuts into an awaiting vehicle.

Nyra's eyes narrowed. She barely held back her snarl.

These were the same kind of humans who'd killed her fathers.

Metal was forbidden in Elphyne. It blocked the flow of mana from the Well. It wasn't so bad in its raw mineral form, but no magic flowed through it when processed. Only Guardians—the ruthless warrior protectors from the Order of the Well—had the power to use mana and still hold forbidden substances. But they were far away from here. Getting a message to them in time would be impossible. It looked like this group of humans was halfway through their job.

A spark drew her attention to a blond, long-haired soldier wandering from the main group to light his cigarette. Dressed in dirty khaki and with his hair tied, the man looked like something dragged from the inkiest pits of the Well. He moved with the coiled danger of a predator. Probably thought he was entitled to do as he pleased because of his brute strength. She scoffed. All humans thought they were entitled to do as they pleased.

Nyra's temper soared when the soldier flicked ash onto the ground. Didn't he realize how irresponsible that was? She should burn his head to see how he liked his furry bits smoldering. Someone needed to teach him a lesson.

Attacking this group was stupid on her own. But maybe she could pester this lone guard... just a little before heading back and sounding the alarm. If she couldn't do this alone, how could she plan to rule the tribe without a harem?

Yes, this would be a good test, Nyra thought. If she failed, she would stop waiting for her wings to create dust and let Colt pick her consorts. At least Nyra's mother would be happy.

CHAPTER
TWO

Sid popped a lit cigarette onto his bottom lip and let it dangle. He wasn't supposed to smoke. The digger's diesel plumes were bad enough that the Tainted fae might learn humans were in their territory. Still, as he took a drag, he found he was out of fucks to give.

Sid was a Reaper—one of the elite squad of fae killers —until recently, when a Fae Guardian crushed his hand and destroyed half his motor function. Now Sid was relegated to patrol duty— *glorified babysitting*—and his perspective on everything had changed.

He inspected the surgical scars on his hand with distaste. He wasn't sure he'd be let back into the field to hunt unless it was a suicide mission. Sid might be pissed off and bitter, but he wanted to live.

Part of the reason he became a Reaper in the first place wasn't to kill fae but to get out of the stifling, crowded, diesel-soaked concrete city. Seeing gray every day did something to his head. He pulled the cigarette from his mouth and scowled at it. He'd picked up the nasty habit while recovering. It occupied his mouth, so he didn't have to talk to people, meaning uncomfortable questions remained unanswered.

Questions like, why did Silver—Sid's ex-lover—leave humanity to be with the fae? Silver hated them as much as anyone, but as a "Well-blessed" human from the old world, she'd developed special abilities that both awed and frightened her. Then she fucked a vampire—the same fucker who broke Sid's hand. Granted, at the time, Sid had just discovered Silver's betrayal, and his emotionally stunted brain couldn't process his feelings. It had confused him. He was about to clock her in the face when her vampire mate crushed his hand.

Sid had never raised his hand to a woman—unless she was the fae enemy. He didn't think he'd have gone through with it. Not because Silver and he had bumped uglies or because she was a deadlier Reaper than him. It was because Silver hadn't been attacking him at the time. His actions had sprung from a place of bitterness...

Silver's betrayal stung. The hit to his pride hurt the most.

He wasn't in love with Silver. Never had been. The entirety of their relationship was to scratch each other's sexual itches, no questions asked. The hit to his pride came from the fact that he should have seen Silver falling for one of the fae. He should have protected her.

Ahh. Who was he kidding? That wasn't the reason either. He wished he could place his discontent solely at the feet of Silver's affair with the enemy, but before she'd even come on the scene, he'd started to see the holes in President Nero's propaganda. Nero said the fae were tainted, poisonous feral beasts... but Sid saw a different story. He saw fae with families. Lovers. Friends. He saw them thriving where humans weren't. The only way to deal with this discontinuity was not to feel at all.

He became a walking, talking killing machine.

Until Silver removed the wool covering Sid's mind. If she—one of the most vicious Reapers he'd ever met— could have a change of heart, then what the hell was Sid doing fighting for an asshole like Nero?

A flying bug knocked his cigarette from his lips. *Shit.* He stomped on it before it caught fire. When he looked up, the bug flew at his face. He swatted, but it dodged his hand, circled, and targeted him again.

"Sid!" shouted one of his team. "Need help carrying this crap."

He glared into the forest, waiting for the bug to attack again. Strange things existed out here. One could never be too careful. What seemed like a bug could be something else. But after one of the workers shouted again, he ducked under a Jurassic-sized fern and walked back to where they were digging up cobalt. His gut churned like the soil caught in the digger's claws.

"Over here," called Brian.

Sid had spoken two words to Brian since the start of

the mission. Now, apparently, the science man thought they were friends.

"We need help carting this to the truck," Brian said, wiping sweat from his brow. "The barrow broke. It's rusted through, so we'll have to bucket the load across."

Rusted through. All the metal in Crystal City was old. It had been smelted, forged, and recycled a thousand times. The only way they'd found this cobalt deposit was through a freak coincidence, but getting out to survey the land had been difficult. And if fae discovered them poking around where they shouldn't, returning would be hard.

It was a smash-and-grab situation.

Carting goods was not in Sid's job description, but he supposed the faster they loaded the truck, the safer it was for everyone. Dumping his rifle, he hauled a bucket of rocks and trudged through the forest toward where they'd stashed their truck. They arrived in Elphyne through a human-built portal machine that used fae *mana* for fuel. They only had enough fuel for one round trip. Everything had to be loaded on the truck, and the digger had to be ready to collect by a precise time, or they missed the portal home.

Sid emptied his load into the truck's tray. He flexed his scarred fist, noting how it hurt less in the wild than in the city. When he returned to the dig sight, he found Brian discussing something with another worker.

"What is it?" Sid asked.

"There's a lot of cobalt here," Brian explained, gaze

darting into the forest. "And I mean *a lot*. If we return with more people, equipment, and soldiers... the supply would help us go a long way in this war against the Tainted Ones."

Sid hadn't taken the time to learn the second worker's name, who wore spectacles and operated the surveying instrument.

"You're saying it's worth a battle?" Sid asked. "If the Guardians find us, it will get bloody. We might miss the portal home."

"It's worth it." Brian nodded. "Every load we bring back means more bullets, guns, and airships. The Professor said that with enough cobalt, we could store energy to power the portal devices."

"We'd better get these loaded then."

Sid shucked off the rest of his weapons and protective gear. They weighed him down. Left in only a shirt and fatigues, he reloaded his bucket, gritted his teeth, and headed back to the truck but stopped as he cleared the trees. Someone was inside the truck. Someone *not* human.

Fairyfloss pink hair flashed about the cabin, then disappeared in a blink. Sid's knuckles whitened on the bucket as he went into Reaper mode. His eyes darted about. His senses strained. The wind rustled the leaves. Insects chirped. The soft sound of voices and the digger floated in from a distance.

And then came the unmistakable buzzing of fae wings.

He slowly put down the bucket but remembered he

had no weapons. He'd removed them to lighten his load as he worked. *Stupid*. He was out of practice. Pink flashed again—this time from behind the truck. Sid didn't think it had noticed his arrival, so he crouched and peeked beneath the chassis. Two dainty, bare feet padded along the dirt on the other side. The hem of a pale gown and the tips of wings trailed behind.

Female.

Normally, he'd be there in an instant to slice her throat. But his eyes darted to his scarred hand, and he frowned. With Silver, his first instinct had been violence, but look where that got him—confused and with a dodgy hand. No. Maybe it was time to try talking first and using violence second.

Straightening, he walked forward on quiet boots. The closer he went, the more glimpses he caught through the gaps in the windows. With every inch of mystery uncovered, he became enthralled with her.

The wings at her back were shaped like a dragonfly's. Light shone through the membrane and cast prismatic light around her. She was shorter than him—maybe five-foot-three. Her pretty heart-shaped face crinkled in thought as she inspected the tires. A thin scrap of gossamer fabric barely covered curvy hips and breasts but then flowed down to her feet. The rest of her gown was made from ferns, leaves, and vines as though they'd grown to complement her body shape and hide the most intimate parts. A flat, taut stomach was on display. A tiny pink jewel winked at her belly button. It matched the glossy color of her lips.

She looked like a fairy version of Cinderella on her way to a ball.

What was she doing out here?

Pieces of her puzzle didn't match the dainty. It started with paint around her eyes that glimmered and streaked down her cheeks like warpaint. It finished with the sharp, piranha-like fangs inside her pouty little mouth.

This pixie was a delicate but dangerous thing.

He'd seen wings like hers pinned in the president's greenhouse at the top of Sky Tower. He'd also heard about pixies, of course. But had never seen one in real life. From what he understood, they preferred to stay in bug size unless visiting cities out of their natural territory, and then they grew to human size to fit in.

This was the side of Elphyne he'd been blind to. He'd spent so much time hunting the monsters while humans raided that he'd not taken in the beauty.

"What kind of magic is this?" she mumbled as she leaned through the open window and poked the truck's dashboard.

Magic? His lips twitched in the corner, wanting to smile. He must have made a sound because she glanced up. Their gazes clashed. Long dark lashes framed violet eyes so vibrant that he was shocked. Like him, she was frozen in place. He should be launching at her, covering her mouth to stop her from screaming... but inexplicably, he stepped backward. He didn't want to alarm her.

"You shouldn't be here," he warned quietly.

His words shocked her out of stasis. Those prismatic wings fluttered so hard they became a blur, and she flew over the truck to land closer to him.

"*You* shouldn't be here," she shot back. "And you shouldn't have been smoking in these parts. You could have set a fire." She stomped on the crunchy, dead leaves. "Look. It's kindling."

He blinked. That bug flying in his face must have been her. He raised his palms. "You're probably right."

"I am?" Her eyes widened incredulously, then narrowed as she folded her arms petulantly. "Of course I am."

Her fangs looked extra sharp up close. And those pouty lips looked extra plump. Like most fae, she was a death wrapped in a pretty package... all the easier to lure prey. They sized each other up. Her violet eyes dragged a slow, assessing path from his boots to his sweat-soaked shirt. Her brows lifted in the middle, and that pouty bottom lip disappeared between her fangs.

Was she checking him out?

Brian burst into the clearing with two soldiers hot on his heels. He aimed his rifle at the pixie. Something lurched inside Sid's chest, and he twisted to face Brian, arms wide, blocking the pixie.

"Don't," he warned.

Brian jerked his gun at Sid. "Get out of the way. She's risking the operation."

"I know," he growled. "I'll take care of it."

18

Just don't kill her.

The thought of her blood soaking into the crunchy soil made his stomach curl. For some stupid reason, he was reminded of Silver. Just a flash. Then he was back in the present and backing up, getting closer to the pixie. Her garden scent grew stronger. Why wasn't she flying away? He glanced over his shoulder and glimpsed a pale face, frozen limbs, and dormant wings.

Fear.

He'd seen that look in the eyes of his kills a thousand times right before he popped a bullet into their head. All fae knew about the magic cutting metal bullets humans used. If she tried to fly, Brian would shoot. She was in her human-sized form and an easy target. Maybe she didn't have enough mana to shrink to the bug size. Or maybe she was just afraid.

He nabbed her delicate wrist.

"Come with me," he growled. "When we're done, you're free to go."

Big violet eyes blinked at him.

"Are you insane, Sid? She'll find a way to escape." Brian retrained the rifle on them.

What the fuck? Sid glowered at Brian.

"Put it down, Brian. I've got this."

"Move, or I'll shoot through you, Sid."

"Brian."

"We can't afford to get caught. We need the rest of the cobalt supply."

The pixie mumbled something under her breath. Sid

strained to catch it, but then he smelled fuel. His gaze swept down, registered the damp soil, and knew the pixie had cut the fuel line during her tinkering. Before his eyes swept back up, before his lips could part to shout a warning, Brian squeezed the trigger.

The gun fired.

THREE

The explosion woke Nyra's survival instincts, jolting her into action. She drew on the last drops of mana in her personal well and shrunk to the size of a dragonfly, hoping she would be small enough to avoid injury from the blast.

Only she wasn't alone.

The handsome human was still attached to her wrist. When she shrunk, her magic flowed into him. He shrunk too. Hot fiery air scalded their backs, and they were thrust upward. As gravity took hold, she tested her wings.

They worked. *Not burned.* Still holding the human, she flew like a drunken *manabee* deeper into the forest. Ferns swallowed them. His weight pulled her balance off-center, messing with her balance. All she could think was to fly... escape the explosion, escape the humans with their forbidden magic-cutting metals. Escape danger. They crashed and ricocheted into plants and trees, slid down fronds, and eventually tumbled into mud. Pain burst in Nyra's back.

My wings!

Crushed. Blinking through blinding agony, little sharp cries burst from her lips. She rolled to a sitting position and the large, flat frond she'd landed on shuddered. Big dew drops wobbled.

The human—Sid, one of the others had called him— had fallen next to her. He groaned and reached for his head. His tied hair was all messed up. The giant frond shuddered again. Dew drops from higher up the frond slid toward them, gathering momentum as liquid collected. Sid's hand slammed onto the leaf as he pushed himself upright, but his quake signed their fate.

Water cascaded onto them. Sid's eyes widened as he found Nyra's. A thousand thoughts passed in a fleeting second. They were too small to withstand the torrent. Danger was coming. Possibly death.

He would have taken a bullet for her if she hadn't accidentally shrunk him.

Maybe it wasn't an accident. Maybe she'd wanted to save him as he'd intended to save her. As the water hit, she thought she might have liked to talk more to this human.

They slid down foliage into the underbrush of the lush forest. Sid's heavier body went faster, shooting past her. He had the sense to grab her so they wouldn't lose each other. She hoped. Nyra tucked her battered wings and tried to protect them, but everything hurt. A bump in their leafy slide shot them into the air. Nyra screamed.

Real panic entered her voice. Without her wings or mana, she was at the mercy of gravity—every pixie's nightmare.

Sid tugged her close. Strong arms enveloped her. Suddenly, her fear became contained in the muscular arms of a human. She clutched his shirt, squeezed her eyes shut, and rode out the dips and turns of their slide, ignoring foliage whipping by.

They landed hard in squishy mud.

Sid groaned beneath her. His chest heaved as he took in great lungfuls of air.

"You good?" he grunted, his voice raspy.

"My wings..."

Nyra untangled herself and scrambled to her feet. She glanced over her shoulder and almost cried at the ragged holes in her membranes. *The coronation ceremony!* How would she explain this to Colt? Or to her mother. The gown was ruined. God, she was so foolish and naive.

The wing exoskeleton was bruised but intact. She would eventually heal in a few days... maybe a week, but until then, she would walk everywhere. If she could shift, then she would heal faster.

But she was empty. Bone dry. Not a single drop of mana existed inside her personal well. Refilling at a normal pace—from nature around her—could take anywhere between hours or days. She would be small for a while unless she found a power source to expedite her refilling process.

With a groan, Sid got to his feet and took in their

surroundings. His gaze snapped to her in disbelief. "You *shrunk* me?"

Nyra scoffed. "I thought that was obvious."

He paled and mumbled, "I thought I just hit my head."

"You did."

"I did," he repeated, shaking his head with a wince.

Nyra reached out. "Here, let me take a look."

He flinched away, and his expression turned suspicious. "You *shrunk* me."

"I saved you."

"Unshrink me," he demanded, stepping closer, becoming more of that predator she'd first imagined him to be.

"It's not that easy."

"Why not?"

"I'm out of mana."

"Get some."

"My wings are broken. I can't just fly out of here and find a power source. It's going to take time at this size."

"How much time?"

"I don't know. Everything takes longer when you're small."

He covered his face with his hand and groaned. Nyra's nerves evaporated, and anger washed in.

"You know, you didn't have to step before me. You could have let them shoot me. So don't blame this on me."

He stared at her, clearly grappling with his choice. Suddenly looking lost, he cupped his nape and shook his head. His mouth opened and closed a few times, but he said nothing.

Guilt tickled her gut, which made her feel worse. First, she couldn't make dust. Now she felt pity for a human. What the Well was wrong with her?

"You didn't have to save me," he grumbled half-heartedly.

Nyra opened her lips, about to say it was an accident, but then remembered that she'd been holding his shirt in fear while he'd gripped her wrist. He'd glanced over his shoulder, seen the fear in her eyes, and then stepped between her and the men with guns.

He'd protected her.

At a loss for words, they stared at each other. The tendon at the side of his jaw twitched sexily. *Well-dammit.* Why did males look so hot when they were angry? She folded her arms, huffed, and glanced away.

Enemies don't save each other.

He eventually said, "I'm Sid."

"I know." Her lips twitched in a half smile. "I'm Nyra."

She had an official title but somehow thought keeping that to herself would be wise.

"You mentioned a source of power," he said.

She begrudgingly nodded. "I need to get to high ground, and then I can figure out which direction to find one."

He gave a curt nod and searched around them. He picked up sticks from the mud. He tested them, discarded them, and then hunted deeper into the plant, where he snapped off bigger branches.

"What are you doing?" she asked, curious.

He glanced at her, then went back to work.

Right. *He's a talkative one.*

Huffing, Nyra checked on her wings. She stretched them with a wince but bit her lip to stop whimpering. Showing weakness probably wasn't a good idea. In fact, she should give him the slip and find a way to get to her coronation. But something stopped her.

You good? he'd asked after they'd crash-landed.

And before, when they'd slid down the leaf, and she'd cried out in pain, he'd cocooned her in his arms. Her enemy had protected her again. When Sid returned with a long stick and a sharp rock, she realized he was still trying to protect her.

"Are you making weapons?" she asked.

He gave a grumble she supposed sounded like a yes.

CHAPTER

FOUR

S id gripped his new spear and tucked the rock
inside a pocket, then started moving through the
mud. Didn't care where. He was sure he'd figure
out a plan as long as he kept moving. The pixie had said
something about needing to find higher ground.

She followed him.

Her little puffing breaths were like fingers plucking his
strings. His body vibrated at any reminder of her feminin-
ity. It took him a few minutes of silence before he realized
why. He'd stopped calling her an "it" long ago. He frowned
and slowed his steps. Was he attracted to her?

"I've decided to help you," she chirped happily. "You're
welcome."

He stopped. Glanced around. Had no idea where they
were. Light barely filtered down into this low area through
the canopy and underbrush. He wasn't sure what to do

even if he located the sun's direction. He was the size of a bug.

There were too many fronds. Grains of sand were small boulders. Ferns were trees. Ants were the size of dogs. At least they stayed away.

With a sigh, he turned to the pixie and raised an eyebrow. *I'm listening.*

"If we want to get to a source of power faster, we'll need wings and—" She cut herself off as if to stop revealing something. But then sucked in a breath and continued. "And I'm not helping you because we're friends. I'm helping you to repay a debt of protection. That's all."

His other brow joined the first. She thought they were friends?

Cute.

Did he just think *cute*? He gave a disparaging shake of the head. She was still fae, and he could be stepped on at any moment. Which meant he needed her help to return to his normal size. He took her hand and shook it, "Deal."

A spark zipped up his arm, and she jolted as if she felt it too.

Her eyes widened. "Oh no, I didn't want to make it official."

Official... Sid's eyes narrowed on their hands. That jolt. *Shit*. He'd just made a fae bargain. Now he had to protect her, and she had to help him. Fae bargains were notoriously tricky, and every Reaper knew never to say thank you or sorry to the fae because they could entrap you. But he'd just gone and trapped himself.

He let go of her hand like it was on fire.

"Oh, puh-lease." She waved him down. "There are worse things than being in debt to a pixie princess. It's not like I pixie-dusted you or anything."

Princess? Her humor died at her last words, and she folded her arms and looked away. *Curious.*

"So what happens now?" he asked. "With the bargain?"

She shrugged. "I have no idea. We'll figure it out when the bargain stops us or makes us do certain things."

"Like what?"

"Like stopping us from leaving each other. Like not helping. Like not protecting."

He looked her up and down, noting the warrior's face paint and fierce fangs. "So that's all for show? You're just a spoiled princess in need of a bodyguard?"

She bared her fangs and snarled, "Come and test me, human."

A thrill zipped through his body. His cock stirred. Was he... was he attracted to that too? His brows slammed down, and he shook it off. No. That would be ridiculous. He'd killed fae. Why would he want to—

"Fuck me," she gasped, looking into the sky.

He cleared his throat. "Pardon?"

"Look."

Sid wrenched his gaze from her lips and followed to where she pointed. Way up high in the tree's branches was a bird's nest.

"That's exactly what we need," she said, grinning.

"I don't understand."

Bright, excited eyes landed on him, and she waggled her brows. "Wings."

"Wings," he repeated, still not understanding, still with half his blood down at his cock instead of his brain.

"We can ride a bird to the power source."

He took a deep breath and glanced up again. The thought of flying on a feathered creature was both exhilarating and a little frightening. He judged the distance; it could take them hours to climb the tree at this size. No harness or rope.

"What if we fall?" he asked.

"We won't. Trust me. I've done this plenty of times before."

"You have wings."

"Which are currently injured and useless," she pointed out. Fear flickered across her face, but she smiled broadly and said, "Don't worry. You will protect us."

He snorted at the idea of breaking her fall but nodded. They had no other options.

Nyra sauntered to the base of the tree. "I wasn't asking your permission."

Each step swayed her hips, sending her leaf and floral skirt jaunting. Nyra started climbing, using gaps in the bark for footing. The tree was more of a craggy tower to him at this size.

Sid put his self-made spear through the back of his collar and prayed the tightness of his shirt would keep it from slipping out. Then he gripped bark and hoisted himself after the pixie.

After a few yards of climbing, he glanced up and realized he had an indecent view up her gown. The gossamer had been torn to shreds, and loose vines caught in the wind, flashing her pert bottom. He quickly glanced back to the bark with his cheeks heating.

"Hurry up," she called, but he couldn't move.

Just don't look up, he told himself. But also don't look down. *Shit.*

What the fuck was wrong with him? It was like everything about her not only plucked his strings but controlled them—wound them around her little pixie fingers. Clearing his throat, he forced himself to look only far enough to locate the next bark to grip. His strategy worked well enough until he caught up to her and inadvertently glanced up.

Definitely compatible with a human, a voice from the back of his mind said. He wasn't sure exactly what he expected fae genitalia to look like but knew it must be close enough to human. Silver fucked one of them, after all.

He might have stared too long at the sheer gauzy strip covering her ass because he misplaced his hand and slipped. Bark crumbled down to the ground.

Get your mind out of the gutter, Sid.

But he couldn't.

For the entire climb, she was there every time he glanced up. Finally, when they crested the branch that felt more like a ten-foot-wide ledge, his cheeks were flaming hot, half the blood in his brain was still south, and he couldn't look Nyra in the eyes.

She sat down and fanned her face. "Phew. That was work. I need a drink."

He was parched, too. But he couldn't entirely blame the exercise. He nodded and occupied his eyes and hormones by searching through the leaves for the sun's position. It wasn't hard to locate as it was setting. Most of the day had passed.

Nyra walked toward the nest at the end of their branch.

"I don't think anyone is home. Ooh. Look. Robin eggs." She caught him in the snare of her violet eyes. "We can hitch a ride when the mama comes home."

"How will we steer it to where we want?"

"I have a little mana refilling. Not enough for us to grow back to human size, but enough for me to influence the bird."

"Won't using your mana deplete your stores again?" He scratched his head, not liking the sound of starting at ground zero.

"It doesn't matter. Once we get to the power source, I'll refill fast."

He peeked into the next at the three spotted eggs.

"There's food right there," he said.

Nyra hit him on the pec. "Don't you dare."

He stifled a smile. "I'd rather it be them than us."

Unable to help himself from teasing further, he pulled the spear out of his shirt. Her outrage doubled, and she climbed into the nest, putting herself between him and the eggs.

"They're babies. Not even born!" She tried to bare her fangs, but tears glistened in her eyes.

"Hey," he said, his voice softening as he lowered his spear. "I was kidding. I wasn't going to eat them."

Her expression crumpled, and she heaved in a breath to steady herself. "You can't joke about things like that to a pixie. It's our job to nourish the forest, protecting all life inside it."

And she was a princess. She would hold firm to that conviction. Now he felt terrible. He fit the spear safely into the nest and climbed in after her. He dipped his chin to meet her eyes.

"I promise I won't hurt them."

She glanced up at him, and a moment of connection passed between them. A moment of weighing each other, noting how fewer walls were between them now than the last time they'd done this. He tucked pink flyaway hair behind her ears, unintentionally brushing her skin. She shivered.

He had the irrational urge to see what else would make her shiver, but he clenched his fist and dropped it to his side.

"We should rest until the mama comes home," Nyra said, somewhat breathlessly.

He nodded. "Here?"

She lowered to the nest floor. He crouched, intending

to fit himself next to her, but the space wasn't as big as he'd thought.

Nyra stretched her legs out and shuffled to the side. "You can fit here."

Sid slotted in the gap between her and the nest wall. Everywhere their thighs, hips, and shoulders touched was on fire. He couldn't think of anything else but her unique feminine smell as he'd climbed after her. Fresh, feminine... same as a human female.

They weren't so different. Nero's lies blinded Sid to the truth, and he felt foolish at having believed them all his life. Even more foolish to have wanted to hurt Silver because of it.

Staring up at the stunning sunset through the leaves, he thought he might be in heaven, which was impossible because he'd sinned so much.

"You're hurt," Nyra mumbled and touched his head.

He winced as she pressed the lump. "I'm fine."

"At least let me check it."

"What can you know about human injuries? You heal fast."

She glanced over her shoulder at her broken wings, then met his eyes flatly. "We still scar."

He exhaled and flexed his fist. "You're right. Are you sore?"

"A little. It doesn't help that they're pinned beneath me."

Without thinking, he pulled her on top of him so she straddled his hips. She made an *eep* sound but didn't fight him. Instead, she melted along his torso until her face was inches from his.

"That better?" he murmured.

She nodded, eyes wide. He couldn't tear his gaze from hers and couldn't tear his hands from her hips. Heat flared down his front... right to where his semi became a full-blown erection.

CHAPTER FIVE

A female pixie only loved her wings being pinned when she was in heat and mated with her harem in the sky. When that frenzied dance came, each male took turns to capture her, pin her, and fuck her while airborne. They called it a dance, but it was a battle. The harem fought over their queen, fought to be the first and last, fought to be the one she remembered. This pinning was how a female created her first dust. It was an awakening, frightening, and empowering all at once.

Empowering because the female used her dust to control the potency and vigor of the coupling. If she wanted it done, she stopped dusting. If she wanted them to take turns with her until the end of time, she would dust forever.

Frightening because if her harem weren't all present during this heated dance in the sky, she could fall or crash. Complete trust amongst the group was imperative.

Awakening because pinning the wings woke sexual needs for both genders. There was something exhilarating about being man-handled in the sky, all agency relinquished, submitting to a harem and their raw pixie urges.

How Nyra had dreamed of having her wings pinned by the right males. How disappointed she'd felt when realizing a mating frenzy would never happen without the ability to create pixie dust. She'd never be the sole object of their obsession, lust, or ultimate possession.

She might be a queen, but she won't be *their* queen... whoever *they* were.

As this man touched her, she realized a loving, trusting connection was something she still desperately wanted. He stirred feelings inside her she wasn't sure she could contain.

Her heart beat faster as Sid's brown-eyed gaze smoldered. Her wings tingled, and a full-body tremble wracked her. More tingles cascaded down her spine, causing her to whimper in need.

Nyra broke his hold on her eyes and checked over her shoulder. Could it be possible? Was that tingle the start of pixie dust? But no... her hopes were dashed when the same smooth prismatic surface greeted her. The membrane was healing, but no golden powdery sheen covered them.

"Are you in pain?" he asked, frowning.

Of a sort, she wanted to say. Reluctantly, she dragged her gaze back to his handsome face. She hadn't expected his raw concern, and it opened her heart.

"I thought I—" she started. Swallowed. Then thought,

what-the-Well. She could confess everything to him because they'd never see each other again once their bargain was done. So she blurted out, "My wings tingled. I got excited because I thought I was making pixie dust."

"You mentioned dust before. What is it?"

"When a pixie finds each mate of her harem, her wings create dust." She wiggled, suddenly uncomfortable. But he tightened his grip on her hips, pinning her in place.

Goodness. She liked how he touched her.

"What does the dust do?"

"It's an aphrodisiac." Her cheeks burned.

His brows lifted, but he said nothing. He also didn't scoff or snap or tease. He just looked at her with steady eyes. So she continued.

"I've never made dust," she confessed. "I'm soon to be coronated as the queen of our tribe, and I'm supposed to find a harem to rule as my consorts. A pixie queen *must* have protection, and she's the central power source for her harem and the entire tribe. As queen, I will have a greater capacity for holding mana in return for nurturing the forest and my people. Without a harem, the power can send me mad or…" She thought of her mother. "Or the power goes, and I fade away into nothingness."

When his warm hand landed on her cheek, she realized she'd been so ashamed that she'd looked away.

"That must feel shitty," he said.

She cocked her head. "You don't think it's weird?"

"That you have a harem?" His gaze turned thoughtful.

"I guess not. It makes sense. It would be best to have protection; one male probably isn't enough. I understand."

"I meant that I can't make pixie dust." She blushed. "When a female pixie goes into heat, she must be continuously... satisfied over hours. The dust keeps everyone virile otherwise there are dire consequences."

"Like what?"

"Like some males die trying to keep up. Or some hurt themselves. Or worse..." Nyra's voice softened to a whisper. "There is no baby and no heir." She plucked at his shirt. "Which is fine if you don't want children, but when you're a queen, you're expected to produce an heir."

"Wait a minute." His brows lifted again. "Go back for a minute. Are you telling me that you get so needy that a complete harem of males isn't enough to satisfy you?"

She sighed heavily and rested her head on his chest. "But not me."

His palms slid from her waist to the small of her back and pressed her into him. "I'm sure it just hasn't been the right time for you. You'll get there."

She smiled against his shirt and plucked at the fabric.

"This is nice," she confessed. "You're nice."

His chest rumbled as he chuckled. "You're not so bad yourself. When you're not baring your fangs at me."

Grinning, she tried to glance up at him but caught an eyeful of his neck, and her smile dropped. It was a strong and thick neck. A vein pulsed with his blood. His jaw was peppered with stubble. He smelled delicious, like a heady mix of musk, sweat, cologne... or soap that reminded her of spice.

Sid's breathing pattern changed. It became shallow, slow. Almost as if he was too afraid to move. Almost as if he wanted to keep her lips hovering right where they were. And then he swallowed, and his Adam's apple bobbed. Her tongue darted out and tasted him there.

She wasn't sure who groaned first, but the rumble between them sent shivers running to every extremity in her body. Her wings tingled again, this time more intensely and lasting longer. Heat pooled low in her belly.

Well-damn, she was so attracted to him—a human. When did this start? She licked him again, testing his reaction. His fingers flexed on her lower back, digging in, but he didn't protest. She licked from his neck to his jaw, where he expelled a ragged breath.

He dragged her up his body until they were nose to nose. They stared at each other for a long, hot minute.

"What are you doing?" His voice was deep and gravelly.

She rocked her hips against him, felt the stiff jab of his erection through his pants, and moaned. "I don't know, but it feels good."

His jaw clenched, and his lashes fluttered as she rocked back. That he was hard meant he was into her too. She cupped his face and whispered, "Do you want me to stop?"

"No." He claimed the last inch between their lips and kissed her. It was never a chaste kiss but hard and demanding and full of hunger.

It hit every button she had. She groaned into his mouth

and kissed him just as ferociously until he gasped and jerked back. His finger went to his mouth and came away red. Wide eyes met hers, and shame flooded her cheeks.

"My fangs." She covered her mouth. "I was too rough."

She thought it would turn him away, that her fangs would be too fae for him, but he surprised her. He dragged her hand from her lips and darted in again, chasing her lips, single-handedly erasing her shame with more of that elicit elixir in his salty taste.

"I don't mind rough," he grumbled into her mouth. "In fact, rough is how I like it."

"What else do you like," she asked.

His eyes caught hers, hesitated. She squirmed with curiosity.

"What?" she pressed. "Tell me."

"I liked looking at your ass as we climbed the tree."

Her smile widened, and she ground her hips against his, aiming for that precious hard length to hit her sweet spot. "Did you?"

He kneaded her bottom and let his fingers slide past her thin gauzy panties. She'd not meant to be galavanting around the forest in them. This outfit was for a ceremony she would clearly miss... a ceremony where she was meant to have a consort picked out. Colt was going to kill her.

There might even be a hunting party looking for her right now.

But Nyra didn't care. Every time Sid's fingers circled further beneath her panties, reaching for that illicit spot between her thighs, bliss rolled through her. She was hardly able to get the next words out. "Tell me more."

"I like the thought of my mouth down there," he whispered harshly into her ear. "Do you taste as sweet as you smell, Fangs?"

"Taste me and see."

She couldn't believe she was saying these things to this human. Couldn't believe he was saying them back. Charged electricity filled the atmosphere. They knew this was wrong, that they were supposed to be enemies, but neither cared. Perhaps they were both outcasts in their own worlds. Perhaps this could be a nice joining of two lost souls. For as brief as the moment lasted.

Sid's fingers claimed the last inch toward the seam of her bottom, slid down to where she was wet, and pressed into that hot damp spot.

"Yes yes yes," she begged as need claimed her. If she didn't know any better, she'd think this sudden, insatiable urge was from pixie dust. But she'd still not made it. This was real. This attraction was all them.

"You want my fingers there, Fangs?" he rasped. "You aching for me?"

His pet name made her pussy clench. She moaned, "Yes, yes more."

He swiped his fingers through her folds, testing, and probing, going deeper each time. Each swipe made her feverish with want. He traced the entire seam from pussy to ass, questing for her instruction.

"Where?" he grunted.

"Anywhere." She rocked against him, mewling as he dipped a finger into her core.

"You're so fucking tight," he breathed. "And wet. You're hot for me, aren't you, Fangs?"

To answer, she smashed her lips against his, then delved with her tongue, coaxing his own out to meet hers. His resounding groan made her chest puff in pride. She loved how he reacted to her. Loved it more than any other lover she'd taken.

What was happening to her?

Her skin was on fire. Her lungs burned. Everything tingled.

And then he gripped her hips and lifted her up the length of his body until she straddled his face. He moved her so effortlessly that she thought about how he would pin her wings if he was in her harem, which was wrong on so many levels. Sid couldn't dance in the sky. He couldn't live with her as one of her consorts. He had no mana. He would grow old, and she wouldn't. His kind had killed her fathers.

But none of it mattered as he worked magic with his tongue. He found her clit, nipped and sucked. Flicked and fluttered. With each swipe and probe, she found her thighs trembling, her heart thudding, and her mind whirling.

Hours ago, she'd wanted to punish this man for intruding in her forest, and now all she wanted was for him to punish her... with his tongue. She hoped he never stopped. He worked her hard and repetitively. And then he slowed like a lover, caressing and caring. Savoring. She submitted to the sensations expanding in her heart and body.

When his fingers joined his tongue, and he said, "Ride me, Fangs," her orgasm exploded through her body like a breaking dam. She gripped his hair and held his lips to her pulsing pussy, doing exactly what he asked, riding him, chasing more of the good feeling. He clutched her thighs and wrung every last drop of sweet agony from her body, lapping and sucking until she was left panting and struggling for air.

She slid back down his body, intending to fill herself with his rock-hard cock, to finish this coupling. She smiled wistfully as their faces aligned again. She rubbed her thumb over his bee-stung and glistening lips. Even more handsome now.

"You were… wow."

"I'm just getting started," he breathed.

But as Nyra went in for a kiss, a screech rent the air.

"The mama!"

CHAPTER
SIX

S id's palm flattened against Nyra's head as the robin
swooped low, its sharp beak clacking loudly as it
passed. The impulse to protect wasn't entirely his.
The bargain.

It compelled him to shield her. He frowned at the
implications of his free will being taken, but there was no
time to ponder. The bird returned for a second swoop. Only
this time, Nyra wrenched from his grip, gave him a chal-
lenging smirk, and leaped upward to grab hold of the
bird's feathers. She mounted it between the wings with
such ease that he imagined she could do this in her sleep.

"How can I keep you safe if you do things like that?" Sid
growled as she tamed the bird with a palm on its head.

She did things with her magic to calm the animal, but
he wasn't appeased. They were high up. Nyra's wings were
still injured. She might fall, and there was no way he could
save her.

"That was reckless," he scolded, feeling anger burn the back of his throat.

"Not done yet," she mumbled, gripping the neck feathers tight and squeezing her thighs.

She had no fear, he thought as he watched her carelessly cling to the twittering and fluttering robin. No fear here in her element, but she'd frozen in front of a rifle. If he hadn't been there... if any other Reaper had stumbled across her...

The robin's head cocked to the side a few times as it considered Sid with an impatient snap of its beak.

"Yes," Nyra said to the bird, smiling. "We will leave you in peace, and my—"

Nyra's eyes widened as she met Sid's gaze. Her cheeks flushed.

"What is it?"

"I was about to say, my mate," she mumbled, her voice a whisper of awe. Then she shook her head and focused on the bird. "Sid will not eat your eggs. I promise."

Mate?

A strange warmth spread in Sid's chest, evaporating the anger.

The robin calmed and then blinked at him, waiting.

Nyra grinned. "Mama says yes. Hop on."

He tugged his spear from the nest and vaulted onto the robin behind Nyra. He adjusted her pixie wings so he wouldn't crush them and reached around her waist to grip the feathers at the bird's neck. This way, he had Nyra caged safely in his arms.

As they took off into the sky, Sid wasn't sure which part of this situation worried him most—that they were flying on a bird or that Nyra had almost called him *mate*... and he'd liked it.

They flew above the forest canopy. Smoke and burning embers signaled the location of Sid's raiding party. He winced and turned away, but Nyra's shrewd gaze reflected the shimmering flames in the gloaming.

"The forest is crying in pain," she said, voice tight. "The explosion was my fault. I had no idea it would be so big."

"The smoke looks like the fire is being put out," Sid said. "The glow is small. Just seems big at this size."

She shook her head. "Will they return?"

Sid was grateful she faced away because she couldn't see the lie on his face. "No."

But she glanced over her shoulder, and his heart lurched when their gazes clashed.

"Good," she said, smiling. "I'll take you straight to the power source, then."

⚖

DARKNESS FELL AS THEY FLEW. Sid and Nyra grew quiet as the wind buffeted their faces. They flew so fast that she would struggle to hear him unless he shouted. It was just as well. He had thinking to do.

Sid should be focused on the fact he traveled to a source of power—a place where mana was rich and ripe for the taking, but he had just spent his evening with his tongue in his enemy's mouth and between her thighs... and all he could think about was returning there. He'd never felt so alive, so full of need and satisfaction. Since Nyra had stumbled into Sid's life, he couldn't stop thinking of her. It was more than attraction or this magical bargain of duty. He'd felt the need to protect her since she'd bumbled around the inside of the truck. She made him laugh. She made him talk... everyone in Crystal City knew he hated to talk. To feel.

His brows slammed down as he recalled his lie.

The humans would be back. The cobalt deposit was too rich, and they hadn't gathered enough resources to consider the mission a success. When they returned, they would bring reinforcements.

Sid's brows drew even lower when he realized he'd called them *humans*, not *his team* or *his people*. Was he distancing himself? Was he already done with Crystal City after giving so much of his life and body to the cause of freeing them from cold isolation?

He glanced at the scars on his hand, gripping the robin's feathers next to Nyra's dainty hand. How he loved the feel of her fingers on his body. How he ached to feel them again.

He'd been angry at Silver for falling in love with a fae vampire... but he'd always known she was different. She'd never told him why she had to wear a metal vambrace while they'd fucked, and she'd never asked why he preferred not to talk or cuddle or extend their sexual releases into a relationship.

He never asked personal questions because he didn't want them asked about himself.

Probably because he'd had doubts a long time ago.

He'd been drawn to Silver because she was the closest thing he could get to that magical life beyond the gray crystal walls... even if she came with a lick of danger. *Especially* because of that danger. That thrill had permitted him to feel *something*. The lack of conversation had allowed him to keep those guilty feelings to himself.

And now here he was, riding on a bird with a pixie braced in his arms. Her prismatic wings buzzed every so often as though she was restless. In the darkness, it made him wary. He hated not controlling all the variables, so the next time they fluttered, he folded her wings and pinned them with his body flush against hers.

Nyra gasped and glanced over her shoulder.

"What are you doing?" she shouted, eyes wide.

"They're in my way," he bellowed through the wind. "Do they hurt?"

She shook her head, returned her wide-eyed gaze to the front, and shivered. He tightened his grip around her to keep her warm. It was cold up here. She continued to shiver sporadically over the next hour of the flight. He was about to suggest they return to the ground and resume their journey in the morning when it was warmer, but she suddenly pointed to something below them.

Craning his neck, he glimpsed an enormous lake surrounded by bioluminescent plant life. This must be the power source.

A sinking feeling grew in his stomach. Soon Nyra will refill her personal well with mana. The magical bargain between them would be fulfilled once she'd helped him return to his full human size. He would have no excuse to stay. No excuse to work through these confusing emotions. The notion caused him to tighten his grip on Nyra possessively. She leaned back into him. He almost buried his face into her sweet, smelling hair, but something heavy collided with them.

A giant screech split the air. Panic engulfed Sid. He used every ounce of strength to cling to the robin, keeping Nyra in his embrace. But the enormous shadow bumped into them again.

"Well-damned kuturi!" Nyra shouted. "It shouldn't be flying at night."

With a lion's body and an eagle's head, the kuturi was a hundred times bigger than them. It most likely had no idea they were on the same flight path. The robin tried to swerve, but the kuturi's talons clipped the robin's wings, and they went down, spiraling. The bioluminous ground grew closer by the second.

They say when you stare death in the face, your life flashes before your eyes. But for Sid, at that moment, he only saw the future he'd never have. The future he wanted in Elphyne with Nyra.

She shouted something at him, but the roaring wind stole her voice. She pointed at her back. *Wings*. He eased back until her pinned wings released. With a nimble grace that awed him, Nyra pirouetted and locked her legs around

Sid's torso. Her wings vibrated so fast that they buzzed and blurred. She shouted and gestured for him to let go of the robin.

Sid had seen Nyra's quick thinking before. He trusted her.

He let go, gripped her waist, and held his breath as they separated from the panicking bird. As with that first time they'd escaped the explosion, Nyra struggled to hold Sid's weight. Gravity pulled them to the ground.

He glanced up, saw fear on her face, and shouted, "Let me go, Fangs. Save yourself."

The whites of her eyes showed, and she shook her head. So he gritted his teeth and steeled himself for the most difficult decision he'd ever faced. He let go. But the little minx's thighs held onto him tighter as she shouted obscenities, angry at what he'd attempted.

Her still-repairing wings rallied and slowed their descent.

Not enough.

They crashed through the leafy canopy of the forest. Twigs and branches lashed their faces, but Nyra refused to let go until they landed on something bouncy. And sticky.

It took Sid a moment to realize they weren't on the ground but still high in tree branches.

"You stupid man," blurted Nyra, a tremble in her voice. "You let go!"

"I weighed you down," he grumbled, rolling to detach himself from the sticky net. "What the fuck is this shit?"

"It's just a web."

"A web?" As in... spider's web?

They locked eyes. Heart racing, Sid wrenched himself from the web but only succeeded in sticking further. Nyra wasn't doing better—her fragile wings were plastered to the silk.

Sid stilled. The net vibrated beneath him like a plucked string. Something was coming.

"Sid?" Panic entered her voice. "I'm stuck and... *Sid behind you.*"

A glance over his shoulder rewarded him with beady eyes glistening in the moonlight. The spider was about the size of a Doberman and balanced along the web with ballerina-perfect legs.

No weapon. The spear had fallen when the robin was side-swiped.

He swallowed.

Fuck being small. He was over it.

"I don't suppose you've refilled," he whispered to Nyra.

"Not enough to grow us."

"Can you do that thing you did with the robin's mind?"

"The spider's mind isn't like a bird, but I'll try." She bared her fangs at it. "Get away from him!"

The spider paused. Then resumed crawling along the web, only this time, it went toward Nyra. Fleeting dread crossed her expression before she hardened it.

"Shield yourself, Sid," she said, never taking her eyes from the creature prowling toward her.

Shield himself? How? He was stuck.

Within moments, bright fiery light exploded from

Nyra's hands and shot toward the arachnid. It screeched as its legs flailed. Everywhere the fire touched, the web melted and broke. Sid started to fall, but another flailing web string stuck to him and kept him aloft.

"No no no," Nyra cried.

Glancing over, Sid caught her flinging hands, but no more fire came out.

"I'm empty again!"

Sid checked the spider. The fire had fizzled out, and it regained control of its senses. Sid snarled and rolled, trying to peel himself from his restraints. Each gained inch was like a marathon run. He wouldn't get to Nyra in time.

But then he felt something hard press his thigh as he rolled and stuck to the web. *The rock.* When he'd fashioned the spear out of a stick, he'd put the sharp rock into the pocket of his fatigues for safekeeping. He yanked it out.

With effort, he turned it in his fist and cut at the web around him. It was a hack job, but it worked. With renewed frenzy, he sliced at the web holding him down. As soon as he freed a limb, he climbed toward Nyra with only one thought driving his actions—*protect her.*

CHAPTER
SEVEN

Nyra had never felt so helpless in her life. No mana. No strength left. No hope. The spider was in kill mode as it crawled its broken web toward her—she could *feel* its need to end her before she ended it.

When they'd fallen from the robin, and Sid had told her to save herself, she'd almost had a heart attack. She couldn't lose him.

On the flight over, he'd pinned her wings to keep her safe, and she'd tingled. The sensation had continued for hours, shivering through her body—making her desperately hot despite the cold. Her wings tried to make pixie dust, of that, she had no doubt. Biology didn't understand appropriate times or logic. It didn't care that he was the enemy. It wanted him as her mate, and it had wanted him then. If she hadn't resisted, hadn't held a piece of her heart back, she would have made dust and maybe even gone into heat.

There had been too many wrong things about that situation. Sid hadn't consented. They were flying on a bird, and he had no wings. They were from different worlds.

But as she watched him claw closer, fiercely cutting the web, furiously aiming for the spider—not her, she thought she might be wrong. He might not be fae, but he knew how to survive in Elphyne.

Sid was ruthless as he attacked the spider. Like his lethal digging machine, his arm dropped on the creature's face, the rock destroying. Then he zeroed in on the spider's weak legs—the ones her fire had scorched—and wrenched each from its body. He didn't stop pulling apart limbs until none were left, until manabeeze popped from its carcass, and he was kneeling, chest heaving, covered in some kind of bug fluid.

He'd saved her.

Sid barely caught his breath before dodging the spider's manabeeze exiting its body. Even he, a human Reaper, knew to avoid the magical life force as it rejoined the Cosmic Well. Each dangerous ball of light had the power to intoxicate anyone it hit. He crawled back to her on the thready web leftovers.

"Hold still," he said, hacking the web around her wings.

They managed to unstick themselves enough to lower to a branch below. Nyra launched into his arms and buried her face in his chest. It was the only way to stop her emotions from bursting.

"It's okay," he crooned and cupped her head. "You're safe."

She squeezed her eyes shut and couldn't speak. From how he repeated his words, she thought he felt the same way. Like his insides would boil if he couldn't get closer to her. Like his heart would shoot out of his ribs. Like he would die if he couldn't be with her.

Both heaving in lungfuls of air, they dropped to their knees and continued embracing.

"You let go," she accused.

He stroked her hair with a trembling hand. "You know why."

"The bargain."

He pulled back and stared hard, his eyes searching hers.

"I don't know," he confessed.

"What?"

Sid's thumb brushed a rogue tear that ran down her cheek. Concern filled his gaze.

"Nyra, I..." His lips closed, and he looked away. "I don't think it's all the bargain."

"What do you mean?"

"Before the bargain, I had the urge to protect you. And there are moments when I feel this compulsion to keep you safe. It's like my limbs move on their own. But other times, the compulsion comes from somewhere else."

"Sid?" She searched his anguished, handsome face. "Where?"

He brought her hand to his heart, then a cheeky smirk as he briefly lowered it to his groin before sliding it back up to his sternum. She stopped breathing and flattened her palm against the thudding muscle beneath. When she braved lifting her lashes, she found wonder and affection staring back at her.

"When you pinned my wings," she whispered. "Up on the robin. I started making pixie dust."

"For me?"

Was that hope she saw flickering in the captured shadows of his gaze?

She nodded. "I had to use every ounce of control to stifle the urge to release."

"Why would you do that?"

"Sid," she breathed. "You're not—"

"Fae." His expression shuttered. He averted his gaze and stood, brushing his hands against his pants. "We should find that power source. It mustn't be far."

"Sid," she protested. But he was already hunting for a way down the tree. She scrambled to catch up and yanked on his shirt. "Sid, look at me!"

He reluctantly met her eyes, but every line of his body was tense.

"You don't even know what I was going to say," she snapped.

"What *can* you say?" He threw up his hands. "I'm

human. You're a fae princess. You need a pixie in your harem, not someone like me."

"But... do you want that?" she asked. "If you had the chance, would you be with me—in my world?"

His resistance melted, and defeat bled into every line of his posture. "It doesn't matter."

"Why not?" She scowled. "My wings wanted to dust you. You, the human enemy. You, my protector. You, the only male I've ever wanted to... well, you get the picture. Maybe I don't need a harem. Maybe I just need you."

"Your people would never accept me."

"You leave that for me to worry about."

"Fangs," he whispered, shaking his head.

Her scowl deepened, and she tested her wings. They felt stronger and healed faster with each passing second. This was the effect of being close to the ceremonial lake. Mana soaked into her from nature at an alarming rate, especially now they were close to the ground. The sooner they went to the water, the quicker it would be.

She let her wings work until she hovered in the air, grabbed his collar, and shoved him off the branch. He growled and snapped his hand over her wrist, ensuring her connection held while she flew them as best as she could to the ground. She couldn't fully carry his weight and probably never would, but it was enough to lower them safely.

After that, it was as simple as following the bioluminescence toward the lake.

They emerged from the forest an hour later. Neither had spoken. It got to the point that Nyra thought her emotions had been high because of the danger. She'd seen warriors overcome with that frantic adrenaline. Seen them come back from a battle and fuck, drink, or get into brawls. Maybe she'd imagined her wings about to make dust. Maybe none of this was meant to be and was instead a coincidence.

She wouldn't know for sure until the bargain ended.

"What now?" Sid asked as they walked across the vast shore to the lake's edge.

Nyra sighed as she placed her palm in the warm water. Effervescent life zinged into her being, filling her with energy and meaning.

"Touch it," she whispered. "Can't you feel it?"

Sid crouched and lowered his hand. Nyra held her breath, waiting for him to respond. When he withdrew his hand with a shrug, her stomach dropped.

"You truly feel nothing?" she asked. "Not even a tingle?"

Sid's eyes skated over the lake, and he cocked his head. For a moment, Nyra thought he might hear the whispers from the Cosmic Well itself. But he shook his head and stood.

"It's just a lake," he answered.

Nyra's shoulders slumped, but she didn't stand to join him. She stayed on her knees and crawled a little further into the water. Her dress was in tatters. The leaves and flowers were either bruised or gone. All that was left was the gauzy silk wrapped around her torso and wings trailing behind her.

"What are you doing?" he asked quietly.

"I'm refilling."

Silence.

"So you just sit there? How long will it take?"

She shrugged. "An hour, maybe two."

The crunching of sand indicated he walked away from the water's edge. But then she heard boots thudding to the ground. She glanced in time to see him drag his shirt over his head. Broad shoulders, defined muscles, and a tapered waist. He had the body of a warrior, protector, of a... consort. And when she looked at him, half covered in spider blood, all she could think was how he'd fought to keep her safe. How he'd wanted to give up his life for hers.

Bargain, she reminded herself and snapped her gaze back to the unending waters.

He returned to her side and sat in the shallows. Every ounce of her being urged her to look at him. Her fingers curled in the wet sand and she stared ahead.

He didn't really want her. This was a relationship of convenience and need; one that would end soon.

I n his boxer shorts, Sid sat next to Nyra and stared out at the vast expanse of the lake. Glimmering lights flickered in its depths, but the most magical sights were outside and on the shore where glowing, buzzing creatures danced. Plants pulsed with holy light. It was magical. Breathtaking. A completely new world.

And a tragedy that humanity wanted to destroy it so they could mine metal and other fae-forbidden resources. He could see how stubborn humanity was now. An entire culture existed here in Elphyne without those resources. This culture wasn't just existing, it flourished.

He couldn't deny that nature was more vibrant here. It wasn't just the bioluminescence but the lushness and the activity. At this small size, he saw life from a different perspective. Bugs, plants, sprites, furry animals, and flying beasts weren't pests he could swat. They had lives, joys, and failures. They shared in this existence too. There was so much more to this life that he never noticed at full size. Alternatively, he could ignore so much more at this size too.

The problems in Crystal City seemed far away.

The societal walls between Nyra and him were nothing.

They were just two beings basking in the moonlight, appreciating the wonder of life.

Nyra had asked him if he sensed something in the water. At the time, he wasn't sure what to look for. He was like a fish asked what it felt like to walk on land. She was disappointed, but it was probably for the best. If he stayed with her, he would only continue to disappoint her, which left him in a hard place.

He couldn't be with her but didn't want to leave Elphyne. This journey opened his eyes, ripped out his soul, and showed him how to let go of those stubborn thoughts. It filled the emptiness that had plagued him. Satisfied the yearning. Half these fae weren't monsters like the president had preached. They definitely weren't tainted or poisoned. There was no disease he would catch—quite the opposite. Here, illness was healed. Just look at Nyra's wings now whole and functional where flames had burned them only hours ago. His hand was still scarred but didn't ache like it once did.

Humanity was the problem... or rather, the current leader of Crystal City.

Maybe Sid could track down Silver. He'd heard whispers of a people smuggling operation that helped unhappy humans escape into Elphyne. He could help.

Maybe he could return one day and find Nyra. He would see her as a queen with a worthy harem. She would see him as an old man. He scowled at the thought and glanced at her sitting morosely beside him. Her sadness was palpable, and he wanted to take her in his arms and erase it all with his touch, to bring her to bliss as he'd done once before.

Instead, he scooped water and scrubbed blood and guts off his skin. There wasn't enough water here on the shore, so he got to his feet and stepped toward the lake. The warm water lapped at his skin like an old lover's caress.

Yes, it seemed to say. *You're here. You belong.*

"Sid," Nyra said, a warning note in her voice.

He glanced at her with a frown. The shore was further away than he'd thought. Water came to his knees now.

"Don't go into the deep," she said. "Or the Well Worms will take you down."

"The what?"

"The Well Worms." She gestured to the open lake and further along the shore to where a jetty and a supply hut stood before the forest. He hadn't recognized the large shape in this small form. "This lake is the property of the Order of the Well, and it's where Guardians are made."

He glanced to the endless depths reflecting a crescent moon. Those whispers he'd heard...

Nyra said, "The Well Worms drag you down into the

deep. They look into your heart and judge your worthiness. The survival rate is low. Very low. Something like three out of ten lives to tell the tale. The rest float, their corpses bloat, their unworthiness a shame for all to see. Apparently, it's a horrific process, and coupled with the low survival rate, not many volunteer to become a Guardian."

Sid stepped away from the deep. He would be one of the floaters with all the fae blood on his hands. He quickly washed and tried not to look at the scarred hand, but it seemed to glare in the moonlight. He was stupid to think Silver would welcome him after how he behaved. Not only had he almost hit her, but he'd continued to work for people who wanted this beauty destroyed.

"You should dress," she suggested when he returned to her. At his frown, she explained, "I have enough *mana* to shift you back to full size. You'll need to dress if you want your clothes big too."

Oh.

That was fast. Ignoring the lump in his throat, he dressed. He smoothed his hair back and retied it into a knot. He scratched his growing beard and then went to stand a few feet from the water's edge where she remained. She wouldn't look him in the eye, and it hurt more than he cared to admit.

"Once you're full-sized, the bargain will be done," she said quietly, studying her fingers.

He gave a curt nod but frowned when he realized she wasn't coming further ashore.

"What about you?" he asked.

"I've only got enough for one of us. I'll stay soaking in the water. It won't be long until I've refilled enough again."

"Then I'll wait."

"Why?" She blinked rapidly as if to stop tears. "The bargain will be over. You won't need to protect me."

She didn't wait for his response. It was as though a bolt of lightning hit him, everything sizzled and zinged, and then he stood at full, human height. Nyra remained dragonfly-sized on the ground.

So tiny.

So fragile.

So vulnerable.

He couldn't leave her like this. Without thinking, he stepped to the side to ensure enough space was between them and then sat. He braced his hands on his knees and stared at the lake.

Nyra's buzzing wings activated, and she flew at him like she had the first time they'd met. His lips curved, but he ignored her squeaky voice until she stopped attacking and flew back to sit in the water sullenly.

The unnatural whispers from the lake were stronger at this size, inviting him into the deep. For hours it seemed he stared, contemplating his options. But it must have been less, for the moon had barely crossed in the sky. By the time Nyra appeared at his side, sitting in human size, he still hadn't come up with a good plan to stay in Elphyne.

Melody, another human he knew from Crystal City, had recently mated one of the Guardians in the Cadre of Twelve. If Silver wouldn't help Sid, maybe Melody could help him assimilate here. Or... he could try his luck in Cornucopia—the lawless city that was neither Seelie nor Unseelie but a place where all fae were welcome. It would be easy to get lost in there. But it all left him with the empty feeling he'd had while living in Crystal City. None of it warmed his chest like the pixie sitting next to him.

"You stayed," she said, digging at the sand beside her.

His scarred hand was inches from hers. His little finger twitched, wanting to reach out and cross the tiny expanse to her. She stopped digging. Their breaths slowed. When her little finger extended, he linked it to his.

"What if we make a new bargain?" he said, meeting her eyes.

"No more bargains," she whispered and shuffled closer.

The heat of her body set his skin on fire. He shivered though he was not cold.

"What do you want, Sid?" she asked, her voice a husky rasp. "If there were no boundaries, no rules, no regrets."

"You," he exhaled. "I've never wanted anything more."

The rightness of his words left him feeling powerful. Invincible. Like owning his desire was all the strength he needed.

"Then claim me," she challenged. "Let me dust you, and the rest will be history."

Could it be as simple as that? Charged energy bounced between them. His heart stuttered, and then he captured her face between his hands and kissed her reverently. Only a second of savoring passed, and then hunger roared through him. He pushed her down on the sand, covered her with his body, and deepened the kiss.

Nyra sighed into his mouth, gasped when he inhaled, and whimpered when he demanded more. Their tongues dueled, and his lips clashed with her fangs, but it only heightened his need to something primal.

"You're mine, Fangs," he growled and then, with a snarl of dominance, folded her wings and pinned them beneath her. He wanted all of her within reaching distance, all contained in his space.

She arched into him with a whimper. So beautiful, his fierce fae princess. So yielding and responsive under his touch. Water sprinkled her body like dew. Full breasts pushed out at him. The gauze was all but gone now. The blush of her erect nipples begged for his mouth. He ran his palm down her neck, traced down the center of her body, and flattened his palm over her stomach.

She writhed and mewled beneath him, but he had her pinned with his strength. That invincible feeling he'd had when admitting his desire compounded and grew. His cock hardened exponentially. She was his, and she wanted him too. He tugged the last of her gown from her body, and then his mouth was on her breast, sucking that hard bud into his mouth, treating it like his favorite dessert.

Her skin was hot and feverish. Buzzing came from her pinned wings.

"Sid," she pleaded, threading her fingers into his hair and holding him to her breast. "I'm about to…"

CHAPTER NINE

"Nyra?" Sid's voice was a distant chime in her mind. She was too overcome with fever to latch onto it. "Are you okay?"

She thought she would create pixie dust for him, but this was more than that. Her skin was too tight for her body. Everything tingled and pulsed with need.

If she needed more convincing that Sid was meant for her, this was it. None of the pixies she'd danced in the sky with had triggered this reaction. And for it to happen on the shores of the ceremonial lake had to mean this was fate.

"Mate," she snarled at him and then rolled them so she mounted his waist.

Freed, her wings took on a life of their own. They vibrated and shed golden pixie dust. For a fantastical moment in time, they existed amid a magical meteor shower. But Nyra was too overcome with passion for marveling. From how Sid's gaze heated and roamed over her naked body, he was about to welcome what it meant to be dusted during a pixie in the throes of heat.

She only hoped he had what it took to survive.

"This is about to get frenzied," she warned, already panting from the hot need building in her core.

"I told you I like it rough," he shot back with a hot smirk.

"You wouldn't lie to me would you?" Nyra clawed at his clothes. Why, oh why did she tell him to put them back on?

"Never."

"Promise?"

"Always."

In a matter of seconds, he was out of his shirt while she worked at his pants. Satisfaction hit when she realized he was so hard that his erection had already pushed out of the waistband. With a snarl, she tugged the damned fabric hindrance down his hips.

She gasped at the sight of him. Hard, long, thick. *Smooth*. No hooked barbs. The shock of it knocked her clear from her mating haze.

"What is it?" he rasped.

"You're smooth," she marveled, running her hand up and down his shaft.

He shuddered in pleasure. "Is that a problem?"

"No... it's... wow. It feels so good. You're so *big*." Prickling heat washed over her like a wave, and just like that, she was back in the needy zone. "After this first urgent release, I want that in my mouth."

With a moan, she placed his length between her thighs and glided up and down, testing the sensation. His smooth, silken, yet hard shaft felt like a dream against her slick, needy pussy. He was enduring like a rock.

Sid threw his head back, gripped her hips, and snarled at the sky, "Stop playing with me, Fangs."

"Then take what you need from me," she snarled back, surprised at the vehemence in her voice. "Use me. I want it."

Fire flashed in his already molten gaze. His biceps twitching was the only warning before she was pinned beneath him. He inched his thick length deep into her core.

"So fucking big," she moaned.

"You can take it."

"Make me."

He took control and pinned her harder when she squirmed or resisted. His hand moved to her lips, neck, sternum, arms—wherever she defied him. Eventually, he slid all the way in, stretching her inner walls and filling her completely.

Everywhere her dust touched, her senses were on fire. She felt every sensation acutely. Smelled him more. Heard his ragged breaths as he slid out of her, and the wet slap and grunt as he drove home.

"Fuck, you're so tight," he groaned.

"S'not me," she whimpered. "S'you and your human dick."

His chuckle disappeared on another thrust, and soon they submitted to the hunger riding their systems. The hard slabs of his sweaty body slid up hers until he angled differently. Sparks jolted through her pelvis. In her veins. Everywhere.

Her climax was a powerful release that rocked her from head to toe. She clutched him, her fingers clawing his back. She melted most deliciously as her mate claimed her, as he gave everything her biology demanded.

Sid's release came in a hard, ragged final thrust as he seated himself and trembled, his face buried against her neck. They were streaked in sand, water, golden dust, and sweat, but neither cared. They held each other's twitching bodies. She sensed he wanted to relish the moment, but her second wave of need was already building.

She pushed him off her and freed her wings. More dust shed, covering them.

"I can't stop," she gasped, her eyes wide.

"Whatever you need," he growled.

"That's what I'm afraid of."

She hadn't meant for her words to worry him, but doubt flashed over his expression before he shuttered it and said, "You are in control. You won't hurt me."

Nyra's need pulsed well into the night. Sid met her pound for pound, stroke for stroke, every single time. They tried washing in the lake, tried removing the dust, but more came. It was like a dam had burst inside her. After all these years of waiting, her body was having no more. It wasn't until hours later that Sid became too tired to hide his response, and it triggered something inside her.

She forced the next wave down, her lungs to slow, her

heart to calm. They were now up near the forest and lying on a bed of soft leaves. The glow from the bioluminescence and moon cast Sid's face into a contrast of shadow and light, and his frown was unmistakable.

"Are you okay?" she asked, slotting herself next to him, trailing her hand down the slick, muscled abdomen to where his still-hard cock twitched at her attention.

He winced. "Fine."

"You can barely form a word."

"It's just that Little Sid needs a break."

She smiled as her fingers wrapped around the marvelous smooth shaft. "I think I can hold the dust back now."

She'd stifled it, but the need was there like a rabid beast barely sated, creeping beneath the surface of her skin. She prayed that he couldn't tell. His lips twitched, wanting to smile, but his eyes remained closed. "You weren't kidding when you said there would be a frenzy."

She kissed the corner of his lips and then slid down his body to wrap her mouth around his fascinating cock. Thick, smooth, veined. His audible gasp made her smile. She licked and laved and showered him with attention.

"Little Sid," she teased, "deserves to be thanked for his service and showered with care one last time."

He thrust gently into her mouth, panted, and squeezed his eyes shut.

"Take it all, Fangs," he rasped. "Just be careful."

"All?" she gasped. "Like, deep into my throat?"

His eyes snapped open and found hers as she glanced up his body. "You've never had a cock in your throat?"

"Pixies are barbed."

"But you have barbs in your soft little pussy?"

"They're not painful and can be quite sensational. There's a biological reason for them, something to do with each male in the harem wanting his seed to triumph, but it means pixie dicks aren't exactly made for my mouth. But with you, I think I can keep my jaw open wide enough without my fangs scraping your precious flesh." She grinned as she took him deep into her throat, demonstrating how skilled she was at protecting his special asset, only coming off him to say, "Which is what makes you so special."

Possessive heat flashed in his gaze. "I'll be the only one who takes your mouth."

When she nodded, he came alive, rallying enough energy for a last few frantic minutes until he climaxed with her lips around him, jetting into her throat and giving a long shuddering exhale before dropping his head back to the ground.

"Fuck, Nyra," he groaned. "You'll kill me."

"Don't say that," she said as he tucked her into his side.

"I'm tougher than I look."

"Yes, you are." She rubbed her hand lovingly over his chest. "And you're mine. There's just one last thing I must do to prove it."

"What's that?" he mumbled, eyes closed again, his breathing evening out.

"Mark you." She sank her fangs into his pec, leaving a bite mark unmistakably hers.

He hissed in shock and pain, but her fangs were embedded in his flesh. Fierce retaliation, need, or possession entered his eyes. He bit her forearm, drawing blood while her teeth were still in him. A strange shift in the atmosphere stopped her from pulling out. She couldn't explain it, couldn't see it, or tangibly feel it. It wasn't a bargain, but it felt magical. This moment was monumental. This mating was real.

She unhooked her fangs and lapped the wound several times to stop the bleeding. When she checked his bite mark, she licked it too. She glanced hesitantly at Sid, unsure if he would have doubts.

"You could have warned me," he grumbled.

"Where would the fun be in that?"

"No more biting," he replied, chagrinned but not angry.

"Never."

"Unless I ask," he said, eyes closed, his brows raised as though he thought himself hilarious.

She didn't have a chance to respond. He was already asleep, exhausted, and sated. And all hers.

chapter TEN

S id woke to the warm sun bathing his nude body, the unique smell of the forest, and a cool breeze tickling his skin. It was early morning, and they still lay on a bed of leaves where the lake met the forest. It was the same blue sky. The same whispering lake. The same lush life.

But everything felt different.

The gray emptiness in his heart was gone, and in its place was a pixie princess with fangs and an insatiable sexual appetite only for him. How could he dismiss the meaning of that? She had an entire tribe of males to pick as her mates, yet her wings never had that reaction for any of them.

As Nyra slept soundly, the curve of her lush, naked body hugged him. Her legs twisted around his as though, even in sleep, she wanted to be tangled with him. His heart squeezed. His cock stirred. After the night they'd had, he couldn't believe he had anything left in him, but the damned fucker reacted despite its raw and abused state.

Down boy, he told it and did his best to survey their surroundings without waking Nyra. She'd mentioned this lake belonged to the Order of the Well. If a Guardian found them here, they might act first and ask questions later. They should get going.

But he couldn't move because then what?

He rubbed his pec where Nyra's bite had left a wound. It would scar, but he wasn't upset. He'd bitten her too. Something about it was so primal and animalistic that he loved it. It felt right in a place like this. Natural. Unlike the scars on his hand, this one left a swell of pride because other fae would see it and know she was his. Mated. He tested the word in his mind. It seemed deeper than any marriage. More enduring.

Nyra roused with a lazy sigh, crawled over his torso, and lazily laved the mating mark.

"Morning," he chuckled.

"Mmm. You taste like mine." She gave one last lick and rested her elbow on his chest to gaze at him fondly.

This sight—this sun haloing her pink hair like she was a goddess of dawn—would be forever burned into his memory. Prismatic reflections showered them as her wings fluttered and stretched. He swept her messy hair from her face, loving how it was like that because of how they'd spent the night.

"You're beautiful," he whispered. "And you're mine too."

She blushed and ducked her head, briefly returning to licking the bite mark and smiling.

"You can't escape me now," she teased. "You know that, right?"

"I wouldn't want to." He held his breath. "But..."

"But?"

His gaze skated past her and landed on the glimmering lake with a frown. "I was so wrong about the fae."

All of his anguish was loaded into that one sentence. His guilt. His fear. His curiosity and need. The whispers crawled to him from across the water as if knowing what was in his heart.

You belong here.

"Sid?"

"I hear it calling to me."

"The lake?" She sat up.

He nodded, and despite the lurch of hope, that maybe the lake had answers to his problems, he said, "I have done bad things, Fangs. There's no doubt in my mind that I would float. These Guardians I detested for being cruel and selfish were the ones who survived the horror of initiation. Not me. If it speaks to their character, what does that say about mine?"

"You think they were all innocent when they jumped in? They had blood on their hands too. We don't know why the Well gives power to some fae and not others. We only know that those emerging from the initiation dedicate their lives to protecting the Well. And, yes, we know that most of the time... they turn out to be good fae." She patted his chest. "But they didn't all start that way. And they don't all end that way."

Was she saying he had a chance? "Have any humans..."

"Gone in?" she finished.

He nodded, but the sadness in her eyes answered him. He was too much of a coward to be the first. Too selfish in not wanting to leave her. He squeezed her shoulder.

"So then I should go to the Order and find Silver. If I beg her forgiveness, her vampire mate might not kill me on sight."

"Why would he kill you?"

"Besides the fact I used to fuck his mate, I also tried to hit her when I found out she'd betrayed us."

Nyra went silent. He craned his neck and found her angry as she traced a finger on his abdomen.

"I'm yours, Nyra," he said.

"But won't you come with me?" Panic tightened her voice as she sat up. "To my tribe?"

"Of course," he said. "That's where I intend to be, but first I need—"

His eyes darted about, searching for an answer.

"You need closure," she answered, cocking her head. "You need to make peace with the one you hurt?"

He nodded.

She bared her pixie fangs. "If she weren't mated, I'd be jealous. And I'd cut the—"

He laughed and covered her mouth. "Don't."

She tugged his hand away. "But you would be, too,

right? I mean. If there was a male from my past that I fucked before I started my life with you. You'd feel—"

A possessive snarl ripped out of his lips before she could finish.

"Yes," he hissed. "I'd be jealous."

Something flittered in her gaze, and he couldn't tell if it was worry, doubt, or satisfaction. Her gaze softened, and she shuffled closer to trail her hands down his front. Something like regret mixed with longing filled her expression. "If we had a Well-blessed mating like your friend, we wouldn't be in this predicament."

Silver and Shade's Well-blessed mating bond had presented as a matching blue, glowing arm tattoo on each of them. From what scraps of intel he'd gathered during his raids and from spies in Elphyne, they'd learned this bond was rare. Only a select few Guardians in the Twelve had the bond in all of Elphyne. Apparently, it had been centuries since another Well-blessed bond presented.

Nyra probably meant that if they had one of these rare bonds, their union would be respected and accepted by fae. But there were many reasons why it would never happen. Each Guardian was mated with a human who had been frozen and asleep for centuries from the old world. He was *born* in this time. He had no immediate link to the old world.

He also had no mana. He wasn't fae. Inside his heart was a cold and barren place, just like the city he'd lived in his entire life. Only Nyra warmed that ice.

"We'll make it work," he promised. "Let's get dressed."

He slipped his pants, shirt, and boots on. He was about to hunt for something for Nyra to wear because her last outfit had been destroyed. But she took care of it by waving her hand and conjuring a woven leaf and vine outfit from her magic.

His brows raised. "Do all pixies wear plants?"

Was *he* expected to? His nose wrinkled at the thought. She read his expression and burst out laughing.

"No, my sexy mate," she purred and rose on her toes to kiss him. "Sometimes, I wear woven or knitted fabrics. And I will be queen one day. You can wear whatever the Well you want."

Thunder shook the ground behind her. With his heart registering danger before his mind, Sid wrapped her in his arms. He glared over her shoulder at a group of pixies landing, spraying sand.

"Did you say *mate*?" snarled a male.

Nyra's gasp caused Sid's stomach to roll. It wasn't a gasp of fear, but the kind that said she'd been caught doing something wrong. The settling sand cloud revealed three male pixies dressed in natural armor and soft linen. Two were warriors. The one with long, dark hair and piercing blue eyes glared at Sid like he was dog shit. The second, who had scruffy tarnished hair and green eyes, looked at Nyra as though she'd broken his heart.

Sid was pleased to see he was bigger than all, both in height and muscle. They might have wings and magic, but he could take them in a physical fight. He thought Nyra was inflating his ego when she said he was big for her, but now he could see pixies were made smaller than humans. He was at least a few inches taller than the biggest of them.

Sid assessed the third male. He seemed regal and aristocratic. His judgmental gaze belonged to a leader, or at least someone used to giving orders. Nero had that look.

A fourth pixie landed. This one was a colorful female with darker skin, rainbow hair, and a horrified look on her pretty face as she took in Nyra's state, specifically who she was with.

"We've been searching everywhere for you, Nyra!" she chided. Then her eyes landed on Sid's chest, to where his gaping shirt revealed Nyra's mating mark.

"Colt..." Nyra said. "I can explain."

The pixie pushed past the males and walked up to Sid. The soldiers tensed, wary, and ready to attack if necessary. But Colt only swiped her finger along Sid's forehead. Then she took Nyra's shoulder and did the same to her wings before rubbing her forefinger and thumb with unreadable scrutiny.

"You dusted for your human kidnapper," Colt exclaimed.

"Kidnapper?" Sid blustered as Nyra said, "He didn't kidnap me."

Colt's expression hardened, and the aristocratic male lifted his chin and said, "You went missing on your coronation day. This human abused you and defiled your chances for a pure royal harem."

"He did nothing. This was my choice."

"You can plead your case to your mother." He sneered

at Sid and then looked down at Nyra. "She will be disappointed that her only daughter is a whore for the enemy."

Sid's fist connected with the aristocratic male's jaw. The smaller pixie rocked to the side, touched his jaw, and glared at Sid as he ordered, "Take him prisoner."

SID DANGLED inside a cage made of twigs outside the hollow of a tree. After he'd punched the male aristocrat, someone had shrunk him. Goddamned bug-sized again. During his disorientation, they captured him and brought him here.

Wherever *here* was.

Some forest. Somewhere in Elphyne. The leaves and trees looked similar to the ones where they'd raided for cobalt. If he had to take a stab, knowing Nyra had probably not strayed far from home when she'd attacked the raid, they were now close to that first location.

The dangling cage was a reminder that he would always be on the outside looking in. He gripped the wooden bars and glared into the hollow where Nyra argued with a group of pixies. From the look of the decor, this was an established royal suite. Luxury bathed the room. Food on the tables made his mouth water. They ate only a few foraged berries and nuts during the night. A manabee trapped in a glass jar shed enough light to illuminate the circular floor that made up the bulk of the hollow.

Colorful cushions scattered about a crescent-shaped bench seat. A female pixie with long hair occupied a throne of leaves and ferns at the center. Her glass tiara had more sparkle than her wings. The bench seat was empty, but Nyra kneeled at the queen's dainty feet.

"He's mine, mother," Nyra snarled, her fangs flashing. "You should understand that a single fated mate—even if he is human—is better than a harem of random males I cannot dust."

Her mother's brows puckered, and she touched her daughter's face. "You have responsibilities."

"You could have picked another harem after my fathers died, but you didn't. You chose to let your power fade."

The queen's eyes flashed. "I did not *choose* to be in pain."

"Exactly." Nyra stood, her spine straight. "I did not choose him. Our bond chose us."

"He is *human*, Nyra," the queen hissed. "The same sort that killed your fathers. He cannot fulfill the requirements of a consort to a queen. He has no mana. He cannot hold it. How can he share the load of this royal tithe from the Well if he can't carry mana? How can he satisfy your needs? You will burn out or fade, and then we are back where we started—with a gully that needs protection."

"He satisfied my need plenty," she replied quietly.

"You... you went into heat?" Multiple gasps rolled over the group, the largest of which belonged to the soldier with tarnished hair.

"Nyra," he blurted, his eyes full of betrayal.

"It wasn't personal, Moss. I didn't do it to hurt you."

Moss and Nyra had a history. Grimy jealously clawed at

Sid, and he wanted to pluck the soldier's wings from his body, but he had to remind himself that Nyra was his. Despite whatever had passed between those two, it had never been as perfect as what he shared with her.

"It won't last," Moss warned, then glanced at the queen, who sighed.

"He's right, Nyra. There is a reason pixies need a harem. One isn't enough, and none is a death sentence."

"Maybe not," Nyra said, still holding to her resolve. "Right, Colt? Otherwise, why would the Well give him to me?"

The rainbow pixie shrugged. "I mean... we won't know unless you break him." Her gaze turned grave. "But if that happens, there will be nothing left of him. Can you live with that?"

Break me? Sid's brows lifted.

"I can't turn back time," Nyra whispered. "I can't reverse what happened. I had no choice."

Moss stepped forward, a fierce look in his eyes. "You had choices, Nyra. They just weren't good enough for you. And that you chose a fae-killing monster over your own kind means you're not fit to lead these people."

"How dare you." She stormed up to him and slapped him in the face. "It was me who went to where they raided. Me who blew up their machine. All me. Not a single one of you was brave enough—"

"Or stupid enough," Moss snapped, barely flinching at the slap.

"—to face that danger."

They all glanced at Sid. The aristocrat raised his voice and said, "But is the danger gone?"

"Yes," Nyra replied instantly. "He said they won't return."

Fuck. Sid looked away. He should say something now before it was too late. It would give them a chance to prepare or call the Order.

"And you trust a creature that lies as he breathes?"

Nyra opened her mouth and then closed it.

As Moss stormed out of the hollow, he gave Sid an unreadable look and hit the cage with his shoulder, sending it swinging. Then his tarnished wings vibrated, and he took off with a buzz that sounded more like the roaring ocean than flying wings.

That single action.

That airborne flight.

It proved Sid had no right to be there, despite what Nyra said in his defense. He would never fly, and they lived at this small size. He would never be able to shift at will, to enter and leave their home as that soldier had done. Even if he could instill trust in these people, doubt would always be behind their eyes.

He was human.

He could lie.

And he had.

He sank back on his haunches and leaned against the bars in defeat. The bars moved. Sid frowned and glanced over his shoulder. When Moss had knocked into the cage, he must have inadvertently opened the gate.

CHAPTER
ELEVEN

Nyra lowered to her knees before her mother.

"Mother," she pleaded. "I don't know how or why, but I feel this is right in my heart. The Well gave him to me. We may not be Well-blessed, but we're something."

"You're confused," Queen Juniper said softly as she placed her palm on her daughter's head and stroked. "If only your fathers were here. They'd know what to say."

"It was humans like her mate who destroyed them," Nyra's Uncle Robin pointed out.

Nyra glared at him before returning to her mother. "Why do you think the Guardians are all mating with humans? The Well is trying to repair this relationship between our races. It wants us whole."

Understanding flickered in her mother's eyes, and then she glanced at Colt.

"Cousin, you are a respected Councillor of the Order. You are in the midst of it all. What do you think?"

Colt frowned at Nyra before answering. "I think trying to understand what the Well wants is like trying to catch air in your fingers."

Nyra slumped.

"But, Nyra may have a point." Deep in thought, Colt tapped the glowing teardrop on her lower lip as she paced the length of the empty crescent seat. It was empty because it was where the queen's consorts usually sat. Where Nyra's fathers used to sit.

"It wasn't Sid who killed my fathers."

But even as the excuse fled her lips, she knew it was weak. He could have. She'd never asked. He promised to never lie to her, but there was nothing stopping him. What if she started blaming him for it? They would never repair their relationship. They would never make the gully whole and nurtured in peace.

But the point remained. She believed the Well brought Sid to her for a reason.

Colt hovered her finger before her lips. She stared at the glowing refractions the blue Mage mark left as she spoke. "The humans mated to the Guardians are not of this time and were gifted with an unending supply of mana during their frozen sleep cradled in the Well's embrace. Nyra's human is of this time, and as such, has no mana. I don't see how this could work." Her gaze landed on Nyra. "I want it to, but logistically, it's impossible."

Nyra remembered something. "He knows Silver. Isn't she one of the Twelve's mate?"

Colt nodded wearily, then rubbed her forehead.

"Well," Nyra continued, "if she could switch sides, how is Sid's change of heart not good enough for you?"

Colt slid her gaze to Juniper and shrugged. "If it were only a matter of hearts, she has a point."

Nyra whispered, "If I have him only for a brief few years, it will still be a gift. It will be better than being lumped with a harem that can't truly share everything with me. That can't help me give you an heir. You told me I needed to pick my dicks, Colt, before they were picked for me. Sid is mine, I stand by it."

Queen Juniper sighed. "The wings dust who they want to dust. We cannot stand in the way of that. It is natural. It is unbidden. Perhaps this human of yours is only the first of an unconventional harem."

"Or the only one," Nyra added, sensing her mother coming to her side. "If it's just him, then I'm okay with that. We've managed to keep this gully safe with your low supply of mana. Who's to say we can't continue to do this for a few more decades."

Her last words caused a lump in her throat because that's all a human life span would afford her. Decades. Maybe less.

"I suppose if he makes you happy..."

"He does." Nyra shot to her feet, unable to hide the hope in her eyes.

"Juniper," Robin chided. "Reconsider."

But the queen's gaze landed on her daughter fondly. "I remember her look, Robin. It was echoed back at me when I looked at my mates. It is undeniable. If this human—"

"His name is Sid," Nyra said.

"If Sid is Nyra's true mate, then we cannot tear them apart. The pain of that loss will be worse than death. And I will not suffer my only child the same agony I've endured."

"But the tithe," Robin pointed out, wide eyes shifting to Colt for backup, but she gave him no support.

This was the queen's decision. "Times are changing, Robin. Perhaps we need to change too if we want to strengthen the gully again."

Nyra launched into her mother's arms and embraced her tightly.

"Thank you," she whispered for her mother's ears only, knowing that a debt could now be claimed according to the fae rules of the Well.

"Don't thank me yet," Juniper said and addressed the group. "I will do my best to retain the crown for a further year. We will give Nyra and her human mate a chance to explore what their partnership means. If this is truly the Well's wish, then Sid will survive the grueling first year." She touched her daughter's cheek. "I know that feverish look in your eyes, daughter. He will need to prove his worth before becoming the consort to a queen."

"He is strong, in both heart and body."

"Time will tell." Juniper's hand dropped, and a sad look entered her eyes. "Go on. Enjoy your mate."

Nyra couldn't help feeling her mother had left words

unsaid. Enjoy your mate... *while you can.* Shoving it down, she turned, intending to walk out of the hollow and release Sid from the cage but was stopped by the sound of her mother's gasp.

It was wrong. *Pained.*

Nyra turned back and found her mother doubled over, her skin pale, a sheen of sweat dappling her upper lip. She ran to her mother's side. "What is it?"

Juniper's glassy gaze met hers. "It's the gully. It's in pain again. I think... I think..."

A soldier ran in, his wings fluttering to give him speed. He skidded to a halt before them, a panicked expression on his face. "They're back. The raiders are back. This time, they have more weapons."

"No," Nyra breathed, freezing at the memory of having one of those metal, magic-cutting weapons pointed her way.

Robin glared at her and furiously spat, "Your human lied. And your mother doesn't have it in her to keep the gully safe."

But he promised he would never lie.

"Sid?" Nyra cried, running out of the hollow. "Is it true?"

But the cage was open, and Moss stood beside it wearing an unreadable expression.

Once, as childhood sweethearts, they used to share everything. He was Robin's son and part of the inner royal circle. She'd been encouraged to play with him. He grew into adulthood as a handsome, strong, and capable warrior. And with his easygoing demeanor, comforting smile, and warm green eyes, how could she not fall for him? They became inseparable. Everyone assumed he would be the first pixie her wings dusted. But it never happened. Eventually, he grew embarrassed, resentful, and ashamed at her obvious rejection.

He was bitter over it, but she didn't think he'd resort to this—her gaze snapped to the empty cage. Whatever *this* was. With her heart thumping in her chest, she asked him, slow and steady, so her fear didn't show, "Where is he?"

Moss raised a brow, and he shrugged. "He made his own choice."

To leave? To run back to his people? To betray her?

No.

She shook her head.

He wouldn't do that.

"Who shifted him to full size?" she asked.

Guilt glittered in his eyes.

"You did," she accused, pointing at him. "What did you say to him?"

Moss's deep voice softened, and for a moment, Nyra believed he had her best interest at heart. "All I did was give him the opportunity. He's the one who asked me to take him back to the lake."

She gasped. "The ceremonial lake?"

Colt arrived at Nyra's shoulder. "I have to alert the Order."

But whether it was for the invasion or because a human dared to initiate in the lake, Nyra didn't get the chance to ask. Colt's rainbow wings became a blur, and she left.

Moss's gaze narrowed on Nyra. "I didn't do anything but give him what he wanted—a chance to be with his mate." Pain flashed in his eyes. "If you had chosen me, I would do *anything* to keep you. I can't blame him for wanting that."

"He..." She couldn't voice it.

"He's gone to face the Well-Worms."

"No." Nyra's heart stopped. As the bustle of activity rose around her, as pixies prepared to defend their gully, her world grew small. Her vision crowded. And what made it worse was that she saw the truth in everyone's eyes. Sid might not have returned to his people, but his lie would spell the end for their gully. He would have known the humans would be back. There was no way the Well would reward him by giving him power. Sid would float.

But he hadn't left long ago. Maybe she could stop him before he waded into the depths.

She bared her fangs, screamed at Moss, and palmed his chest to move him out of the way. He staggered and fluttered his wings to stop falling from the branch. She launched into the air, wishing that she missed the last of his words.

"Go to him, and you're choosing him over the gully."

It wasn't until she was a few minutes into the journey that she realized someone must have flown Sid to the lake, and it was a few hours away. Moss had a second pixie helping him, or he'd used a portal stone to transport Sid there instantly. And if that was the case, no matter how fast she flew, she wouldn't arrive in time to stop him.

Her wings faltered. Gravity pulled her down. A hand clasped her wrist and lifted, helping her regain equilibrium. Nyra looked into Colt's eyes.

"I thought you left," Nyra gasped.

"I did. And then I realized you were probably headed in the same direction, and you might want to get there faster than your wings can travel. I have a portal stone." Colt gave her a small smile as she held the smooth, small stone in her palm. "You were right when you said the Well works in mysterious ways. There have been too many strange coincidences with your story. If what you say is true, if he's your one true dick, I'll take you with me."

"Even if I should be defending the gully?"

Colt's eyes met Nyra's. "Even then."

CHAPTER TWELVE

S id floated in the lake, staring at the sky as the sun
dipped beyond the horizon, and it turned from
blue to teal to orange and navy. He tried to come to
terms with what had just happened. Was he yet to wake
from a dream or reality or a nightmare?

The lake no longer called to him.

When Moss had portaled him here, Sid had waded into
the water without hesitation. Only a prayer existed in his
heart.

Help me belong. Help me protect.

He'd waded into the deep, his legs treading water, and
he'd waited. Nothing. No answer to his prayer. No worms
rising from the deep. Nothing.

Now the gloaming was starting to fall like a smoth-
ering blanket with little fiery holes poked through it. All he
could think was that Nyra's tribe was right. He was human.

He was empty. He wasn't even worth judgment. The divine ignored him.

This cold indifference from their revered Well was Sid's reward for his selfishness. He wasn't even afforded the shame-saving ending of not being alive to face his rejection. That cowardly end hadn't entered his mind before now. He'd just wanted to be with Nyra, to finally give in to that guilty notion that he could belong here in Elphyne.

That he'd been wrong.

That he wanted to make up for it.

He might have floated there, staring at the twilight for hours, minutes, days, thinking about his options. In the end, he came to the conclusion that if the Well wasn't going to help him gain absolution, then he had to take a page out of Nyra's book and do it himself. He would swim back to shore, find Silver, and join in her fight. He knew how Reapers worked. He knew how they fought.

He didn't need mana to protect this world.

He didn't need permission.

All he needed was—*something brushed his ankle.*

Sid's wet skin prickled with alarm. He tried to silence his movements and hear the danger coming. But the sound didn't come from beneath. It came from across the water, from where Nyra flew toward him, screaming for him to get out.

He tried to wave and say that he was okay, that the worms didn't want him anyway, but that *slither* hit his foot again. Then his hand. Then it wrapped around his neck like a noose and dragged him down. The last thing he saw before going under was the flare of Nyra's pink hair and wings moonlit like an angel.

∮⚖️◊

SLICK, oily darkness consumed Sid as he was pulled down, down into the deep. Down so far that the light of the moon extinguished. Down so far that there was no hope for him to rise and find air again.

Something like fear ripped through him—not because of the burn in his lungs, or the twisting, slithering lengths squirming around his body—but because Nyra had seen him go under, and he'd caught the tragedy in her eyes. She didn't think he would survive.

Maybe that was why he resisted the slithering things trying to gain access to his mouth. Maybe that was why he panicked when he felt them everywhere, inside his clothes —trying to violate him in horrific ways without his consent. His instinct to survive kicked his legs, made him buck and thrash and mindlessly beg.

But he gave permission, didn't he?

That's why he was there. To submit to being judged. To answer the call. To belong.

He stopped struggling. The burn, the suffocation of the worms, became so intense that he suddenly stopped feeling at all. There was no emotion, no sensation. He floated in a dark weightless space, wondering if this was the calm before death often spoken about. That moment where they saw a light at the end of the tunnel... or the darkest pits of hell.

No.

This moment of floating peacefully wasn't hell.

When the worms breached him, searching him inside and out, hunting for whatever it was they hungered for, he thought—*this* is hell. Not because he deserved the agony, but because he never got the chance to tell Nyra he loved her.

⚖

SID'S EYES fluttered open to darkness. But air. Sweet, glorious air dragged in and out of his abused lungs. He was wet. Water somewhere lapped against the shore. But he was not *in* the water.

And it whispered. *You're here. You belong. You are ours.*

With a ragged, choking gasp, he jackknifed up.

"Sid!" Nyra's strangled voice came from his right.

His head swiveled in the dark to find her crawling toward him on the shore, her golden skin luminous, her prismatic wings like diamonds sparkling in the night. He flinched at the brightness.

He was at the lake. No longer in it, but spit out on the shore. Deep night had fallen and now his eyes adjusted to see remarkably well. How long had he been out? How much time had passed?

And why the fuck did everything seem so vibrant? It was

night. He knew it. But he felt like he could see almost as if it were day. The air tasted sweet. The ground sparked a sensation against his skin. Nyra scrambled toward him, shouting over her shoulder as she crawled, "Colt! Colt, come quickly!"

She threw herself at him, bowling into him until they fell against the sand. God, even her warm skin was hard to describe. It was like she'd been standing by the fire... no—he ran his hands over her smooth body—it was like the fire was now in him.

She clutched his jaw between her hand and peppered his face with kisses. "You stupid, dumb, amazing, dumb and..." Anger and fury contorted her pretty features. "You lied to me! You broke your promise."

"I'm so sorry. I—" He shook his head as shame threatened to overwhelm him. "I fucked up and I was too much of a coward to tell you. An apology wasn't good enough. I had to prove it."

She pulled back, her eyes narrowing on his face.

He lifted his thumb to smear a glob of blue bioluminescence from her cheek, but it wouldn't move. He blinked, trying to focus. It wasn't on her tear-stained cheek. It was a reflection... of light cast from his.

"Sid," she breathed, gaping at him in awe, touching a spot beneath his left eye with reverence. "You have the Guardian mark."

Did it work? His hand flew to his face to see if he could feel it. His gaze darted to the lake, searching for evidence of what had happened. Of his acceptance. But those whispers were silent again.

Sand exploded as another pixie landed next to Nyra. She held out her hand, and a glow illuminated above her palm as if she held a firefly or manabee... but it was magic... and Sid could sense it as though he and it were made of the same stardust.

"Colt," Nyra said, reluctantly scrambling off Sid. "Look."

Colt's eyes focused on Sid's cheek, and she smiled. He glanced at her lower lip, where the same blue teardrop twinkled. A Mage of the Order of the Well. That made him...

"Congratulations, D'arn. You are the first human in the history of Elphyne to survive the Guardian initiation."

"What did you call me?"

"D'arn. It is the official title of a Guardian," she explained, glancing around the sand as she continued. "It precedes your new Guardian name. But I don't see a name in the sand. Most of the time, the Well Worms spit you out with a new name."

"My name is Sid," he said, his throat still raw from the invading worms. "Sidney."

She smiled. "Well, I guess you'll remain as Sid unless you choose a new name—a rarity but not unheard of. There have been a few other Guardians who claimed their new identities. But there will be more time for deciding that later during your training."

"Training?"

She cocked her head. "As a Guardian, of course. You will now be amongst the select few who can hold forbidden items and still access your mana." When he continued to look dumbly at her, she explained. "You have mana, Sid. You will have to learn how to harness that gift and how to fight to uphold the integrity of the Well."

"Of course," he mumbled. But his eyes shifted to Nyra. He didn't want to leave her side. She reached for him.

Telling Colt that he refused to go to the Order was on the tip of his tongue when she said, "You won't be the first mated Guardian. But you will have to train before you can return to your mate. The council will decide the rest of your fate, and I can put in a good word. Nyra is family, but there are five other Councillors in addition to the Prime who will decide your fate. Oh, look. Here's another Councillor now. I believe you may have met him already—D'arn Shade."

Two bodies emerged from a cloud of shadow further down the shore.

That Sid could even see the shadow amongst the impossible night again proved that he was different inside. With this new clarity, he noticed shadows gather like a storm cloud and then release its inhabitants—one male, one female.

"Silver," he rasped, getting to his feet, his heart lurching.

This was the moment. He could make amends for hurting her. But would she let him atone? Would her dangerous vampire mate allow it? Sid kept his wary eyes on the dark-haired, obscenely handsome vampire as he stalked closer. The shadows followed him and folded around his black leather Guardian battle uniform. Vampiric wings unfurled behind him and Silver as they approached, almost languidly, almost like a sleepy cat stretching when sensing a rival amble by, plucking at the ground in a veiled warning—*See my claws. See my wing span. See, I am an apex predator.*

Silver was named for her long silver braid. He used to think it was because of the silver vambrace she always wore around her forearm, but now he could see it was more. No silver or metal clung to her as far as he could see. She was in complete control of her fearsome power, and the color in her bronzed cheeks brought a beauty he'd never seen.

Sid's eyes slid to Shade. He was the reason for Silver's happiness, just as Nyra was the reason for Sid's.

Nyra hissed and bared her fangs. She stepped between him and the approaching couple. Sid sensed her possessive defenses slam up. Nyra's mating mark on his chest burned, and he felt the need to protect her as if that fae bargain still jolted his body into action. He placed a palm on her shoulder and tugged her back to him, silently folding her wings and keeping them dormant between them. She shivered, and goosebumps erupted on her skin, but she settled against him.

"My my," Shade drawled, his voice smooth like whiskey. He looked Sid up and down. "How the tables have turned."

"Sid?" Silver gaped.

She stepped forward, but Nyra gnashed her fangs, and

Shade halted his mate. "Careful, darling. You're about to walk toward a newly mated pixie."

"Mated?" Silver's eyes darted between Nyra and Sid, then to his left eye. "Fuck, Sid. You have a lot to catch me up on." But then she grinned widely and breathed, "You fucker. You're here."

"I'm here," he returned, his lip twitching in amusement, and he wasn't sure why, but he nodded to the pixie at his front and proudly announced, "This is Nyra, my mate."

"*Princess* Nyra of Athyrium Gully," she corrected, never removing her glare from Silver.

With a smug look, Silver hit Shade's chest with the back of her hand. "See? You wanted a reason not to kill him. Ask, and the Well shall provide."

"Hmm." Shade turned his shrewd gaze to the pixie still baring her fangs at his mate. "Fuck with her, pix, and you will have me to deal with."

"Fuck with him *again*, vampire, and I will bite your dick off before feeding it to the worms."

Shade roared in laughter. Silver's smile stretched, and she met Sid's gaze. "I like her."

"I..." Sid's voice died in his throat as Nyra's hand wrapped possessively around his. He glimpsed the scars still running over his knuckles. This was why Nyra was defensive. He met Silver's gaze, to apologize for almost hitting her, but Silver stopped him with a shake of her head.

"It's in the past," she said. "You're in Elphyne now."

"And we have more pressing issues to deal with," Shade said as more Guardians and representatives from the Order arrived. Some came by wings, some by portal, and some by foot. Shade glanced over his shoulder, his eyes locked on a regal, white-winged and haired woman with dark skin as she strode across the sand. Then he met Sid's eyes. "If you want to defend your mate's gully, we must go before the Prime arrives and demands you stay."

"He's right," Colt confirmed. "She will insist you stay and leave the fighting to others."

Shade held Sid and Nyra while Silver grabbed him, and then he muttered, "Let's hope this works."

His shadows threw ribbons of darkness around them and turned everything black.

THIRTEEN

Nyra's scream muffled as a hand slapped over her mouth and the shadows around them faded. They weren't at the lake anymore, but in a forest with random gunfire peppering the air. Moonlight shone down, illuminating their environment enough to tell her where they were—near her home and where the humans were raiding.

The vampire Guardian had somehow portaled them through shadows. He let go of her mouth and glanced at Sid, who braced a tree and gathered his breath.

"It takes some getting used to," Shade explained quietly.

Silver crouched next to Nyra. "While Sid's gathering his breath, what can you tell me about the humans who were here before?"

They listened intently as Nyra relayed everything she'd observed the last time. When she got to the bit where she exploded the truck, Silver smirked. Her gaze softened when Nyra told how Sid had protected her.

"I always knew he was a good man," Silver said. "Like many humans, we're just misinformed."

Sid joined them after a moment, wiping his mouth. He must have vomited. Even in the moonlight, he still looked green in the face. But he rallied and said gruffly, "They had rifles. Brian said the deposit was too rich for them to ignore. I imagine they brought reinforcements."

Silver nodded grimly. "There will be more Reapers and weapons. Nero is getting desperate."

"I'll get a closer look," Shade said as shadows ribboned around him, hiding his form.

In seconds he was indistinguishable from the darkness. Must be gone.

"Your tribe," Sid said to Nyra, worry in his eyes. "That gunfire must mean they're attacking."

Fear stabbed Nyra's heart. "They won't be able to survive the bullets. And they will all be low in mana supply."

He swallowed. "I don't know if I have any power."

"You won't need it, Sid," Silver reminded him. "You can hold metal and still stay connected to the Well. As someone who was not born with powers, the one piece of advice I can give you is that if you feel the urge to release something, do it. Just send that release at them, not us."

The haunted look in her eyes told Nyra there was more to that story.

He nodded grimly but didn't look convinced. Still, he

turned to Nyra and said, "I don't suppose I can convince you to stay out of sight?"

Her smile was more a baring of the fangs. "I can hold my own. And besides, the skill to shrink and enlarge at will is handier than you realize. Remember when the blast hit, and I shrunk us?"

He nodded, eyes intently on her as she finished.

"I can use opposing forces to balance each other out or to make a bigger impact. So if I'm small, and punch the enemy as I grow, the force will be tenfold."

Sid's eyes lit up with understanding. Something like pride shone back at her before that worry dropped in again. She felt the tug to protect deep in her heart, so she whispered, "I'll be safe."

Shade returned and conveyed the location of the humans—and that the pixies were outnumbered and outgunned. Any time one of them grew big, someone fired their gun. All it took was a little bullet to hit the pixie anywhere, and their magic was cut off.

An explosion thundered the ground, shaking the trees. Nyra thought, perhaps, it was from another machine blowing up, but then she felt a strange scream in her bones.

She gasped, "The earth is in pain."

Shade cupped his mate's cheek and said, "Darling, if you need to unleash to save yourself, we will worry about consequences later. Understood?"

She gritted her teeth but nodded.

"Good." Then his shadows stole him again.

"Let's go," Silver said, straightening. "Sid—"

She used some kind of hand gestures to signal to him. He nodded, signed something back, and the two of them moved like soldiers in the same unit. It reminded Nyra of watching Moss and his soldiers move in tandem during training exercises. They really did have a history, but it wasn't to Silver that Sid looked as he delved into danger. He shot Nyra a glance and then made a pinching sign with his fingers to her—*Shrink. Be safe.*

She grinned. Having been at a power source for the past few hours, she was filled to the brim with mana. Shrinking felt like it barely touched her reserves. She was dragonfly size in a heartbeat and, following the glow of the fire, she flew into the fray. Nyra didn't count on the pain she felt from the forest affecting her judgment, but it was there, begging her to help as she rounded a tree near the clearing.

Scorch marks still existed from the fire she'd caused. A charred, rusty shell of a vehicle sat in the center. But the main fight was further down where they'd been collecting their resources. A glimmer of tarnished pixie wings shone in the brief gunfire. Nyra glimpsed Moss, his face furious as he materialized behind a human and sliced his throat with a bone knife. Before the human fell to the ground, he was gone.

That's what she should be doing. Nyra was about to search for a weapon when her mother's strained voice stopped her.

"Nyra..."

She whirled and searched the dark forest. She found her mother kneeling on the charred ground, surrounded by a ring of guards. She looked pale... her wings even duller than before.

"Mother." Nyra flew down to meet her, landing on soft and sure feet.

"Your duty is here, daughter." Juniper drove her fist into the dirt, gritting her teeth. Power bloomed beneath them. Charred dirt and soil turned, making way for fresh shoots of saplings to grow.

"While they fight," Juniper said. "We ensure it's not too late for the gully to recover. If we wait too long, there is nothing to call on. No mana to rise to the surface and fill the saplings with new life."

"We have to repair the wounds before they are deadly," Nyra said, understanding.

Her mother gave her a curt nod, then together, surrounded by a guard, they went from broken tree to burned plant to injured wildlife. They used what mana they had to help restore the life the humans had stolen. But no matter how much they tried, it didn't seem enough.

Saplings would sprout only to wither. Fires were put out, only to catch again further down when the wind blew.

"My connection to the Well fades," Juniper moaned.

"It's the metal they're mining, Mother," she said. "It must have been disturbed enough to stop the flow. Or maybe it's their machines and weapons in the same place."

"It will affect how mana flows in this area," Juniper confirmed.

"There is a Guardian with us," Nyra said. "And Sid. He... he made it, Mother. He emerged from the lake a Guardian."

Hope flared in her mother's eyes. "You were right. He has a good heart."

"But how can he—they—help?"

"I don't know, but..."

"I'll find him."

Before her mother could stop her, Nyra launched upward and flew in the direction Sid had disappeared. She was shocked to see so many soldiers scurrying between the trees—both human and fae—fighting.

"An army," she breathed, her blood draining. "They brought an army."

FOURTEEN

More humans were here than Sid had guessed. Maybe fifty. Maybe more. A few Reapers were among them, but not too many. That was a good sign. It meant either Nero was running low on elite soldiers, or they were busy elsewhere.

With the help of Shade and Silver, he arrived in time to fight with the pixies for the gully—which he realized now was only a small part of a greater whole. The woods outside Crystal City were a dead wasteland. He could see now, without a doubt, the greed and use of harmful and dangerous substances by humanity had poisoned the earth. The further they spread, so did the disease.

A black-clad soldier with goggles and a mechanical gun stepped from behind a tree and hesitated when he saw Sid. That small pause was all Sid needed to steal his weapon, clobber him over the head, and then unmask him.

Blond hair. Wild eyes. Youthful face.

"Jimmy," Sid murmured.

The kid was fifteen when Sid had seen him last. Jimmy had chased Silver and Sid on their fateful Reaper mission into Elphyne to kidnap a powerful fae child for Nero to exploit. Sid's heart clenched at the memory. Jimmy was a frightened teen with pimples and was a helluva lot greener than now.

Stronger jaw, haunted eyes, broader shoulders.

Jimmy had only followed them because he'd needed medicine for his mother... or was it his sister? Sid shook his head, ashamed at his lack of memory.

"What are you doing here?"

"You're one of *them* now." Jimmy glared at Sid's blue mark beneath his eye. "You're a fucking Tainted."

Sid crouched to grip the young man's collar. "Listen carefully, Jimmy, because I will only say this once. There's a reason Silver and I switched sides, and it wasn't from some fairy spell. Nero lied to us all, you hear me? We don't need to be trapped in that cold prison. Your mother wouldn't be sick out here. Or, at the very least, she would have access to healers."

"I don't want to turn into a fucking animal."

"Do I look like an animal?" he growled, feeling frustration build when he thought of Nyra, how she had wings sprouting from her back, how other fae animalistic sides were different to humans but not something to be feared. "Even if I did look it, some of these fae—these *tainted animals*—act more human than us."

Silver appeared next to him. Perhaps she heard a

familiar voice, or this was fate or the Well at work. But the second person Jimmy recognized broke his composure. He tried to hold it back, but Sid saw the doubt in his eyes.

"Jimmy," Silver said softly, kneeling next to him. "Go back to Carla. Go back to Polly, and tell them quietly that you can come here and you will be welcome."

"But..."

"I know you were with the party that kidnapped Willow. We've all done bad things we regret. That Sid is standing there before you now, his slate wiped clean, means you all have a chance. Don't be a fool like these others. It will get you killed, and then who will look after your mother and sister?"

Emotion flared in Jimmy's eyes, and Sid knew Silver had him. She lowered herself, whispered something into his ear, and then let him go. Jimmy scrambled to his feet, gave them a confused and pained look, then disappeared into the dark forest.

"Everyone counts." Silver slid her bleak eyes to Sid. "If we can spread the word, then the more humans we can convince to leave Nero, the better for everyone."

"I hope you're right."

Because if Jimmy goes back to tattle on them, anyone they befriended in Crystal City could be dead.

A scream behind Silver, somewhere nearby in the forest, said the battle still raged. Silver kicked Jimmy's discarded mechanical gun toward Sid with a wince. "I can't carry it without breaking my connection to the Well. But you can."

Realization hit him—he could fight Nero with his own weapons. They jogged into the fight. Any human he came across, he gave the same choice he gave Jimmy. Retreat. Go back and spread the word that Nero has lied. If they refused, he gave them a swift death.

He almost thought they were winning, that they'd successfully stopped the raid before it worsened, but then he walked into the clearing where the digger was frozen, its claw buried in the dirt. Two trucks were filled with raw cobalt. More Reapers and raiders had formed a barricade, protecting their spoils.

Some were Sid had given a second chance only minutes ago. They'd promised to return to Crystal City. Their betrayal hit him like a knife to the heart. He scanned the group, desperately seeking that shock of blond hair, and couldn't find it.

At least Jimmy had the sense to leave.

Shade stepped out of the shadows, his expression grim as the humans gathered their weapons and prepared for an assault.

"Fuck them," Shade growled, his vampiric fangs flashing. "Silver darling, let me drop you in there, and you can unleash."

"That's irresponsible," she snapped back at him. "You know the decay can spread from them to the wildlife around here."

"I'll contain it with my darkness."

She considered it. But in the space of a blink, she thought too long. The humans had recovered, reloaded their weapons, and started spraying gunfire randomly into the bush around them. Panic scorched Shade's face. He grabbed his mate, and they disappeared in an explosion of shadow. Sid ducked behind a tree and held his breath. As he stayed shielded by the tree, he would be—

"Sid!" Nyra's voice was a hammer to his heart.

Time stood still. Nyra as behind him, full-sized and not shielded by a tree. He heard the *pop pop pop* of gunfire. The whiz as bullets sailed past their heads. Power built inside him—something born of instinct, fear, and the urge to protect—he grabbed his mate and unleashed. He tried to do what Silver had said and pointed it away from them... but the power didn't want to listen. It stayed around Sid and Nyra, and suddenly, they were no longer human size. Their bug-sized bodies tumbled across the ground as bullets splintered into the tree behind them, cascading shards of wood like boulders.

He covered Nyra with his body, "Stay down."

The gunfire suddenly stopped. Either they'd run out of ammunition or—screams filled the air. Wet gurgles. Horrific cries for help. Sid heard someone gulping and drinking and remembered Shade was a vampire. Human blood was extra tasty.

Shade had done what Sid did—protect his mate first. Then he returned to make them pay.

Sid climbed off Nyra. "Are you hurt?"

She shook her head, wild eyes flared as he helped her to her feet.

"You shifted us at the right time," he said, praising her. "Can you grow us again so I can join Shade?"

"But Sid, I didn't shrink us."

"What?"

She cocked her head, studying him. "That must have come from you."

His finger touched the spot on his cheek where the Guardian teardrop glowed. "Do you think it was my gift? You always talk about your mana depleting after you use it, but I feel the same. Am I supposed to feel different?"

Her lips turned into an O of surprise, and she patted herself. "I feel different. I feel like I shifted, even though I didn't command it."

"You think I borrowed your mana?"

"Or maybe..." Her gaze turned thoughtful as it landed on the metal weapon in his hands. Before he could stop her, she snatched it from him and gasped, her eyes wide and panicked. He thought she'd drop it, but then one hand latched onto him, and she exhaled in relief. Excited eyes met him, she gripped his arm and said, "I'm going to shift us back to full size."

"But you can't," he said. "You're holding the gun."

In a dizzying instant, they were back to full size. Nyra grinned and handed him the gun.

"Your gift is sharing," she exclaimed. "Do you know what this means?"

"I don't have a gift?"

"It means that when we touch, you can borrow from me, and I can borrow from you. I could use mana while holding metal, but only when connected to you. My connection to the Well was cut savagely when I let go of you. It felt like I'd flown too high or had walked over ancient ruins. It hurt, Sid. It hurt to be cut. But then I touched you and it was back." Awe filled her eyes. "You're the answer to the gully's problem."

"Fangs, I'm not following."

"My mother is having trouble connecting to the Well with all this metal." She gestured to the mined and spilled cobalt. To the bullets littered over the ground. To the trucks. "But if I'm connected to you, borrowing your gift to flow the mana around the metal, then I can do what she can't. I can repair the damage the humans have done. I can bring the gully back to life."

Sid could virtually feel the joy bursting from her. He lowered his lips and kissed her. She smiled and pulled back to say, "I'll get my mother. We'll start here where it's worse."

She was gone before he could protest, so he took a breath and shook his head, smiling to himself at how happy she was. His smile dropped when he walked toward Shade and Silver at the heart of the mining operation.

They had the situation under control. Those who weren't dead were divested of weapons and huddled in a circle. Five, Sid counted as he walked closer.

Manabeeze floated lazily around the clearing, leaving ghostly streaks of light swirling through the misty darkness. Fae had been killed—Nyra's people. His heart squeezed.

Shade's hand rested protectively on Silver's neck as she leaned over the group, snarling words at them Sid couldn't hear. Shade didn't seem worried. His dark gaze eased to Sid as he approached. His pointed vampire tongue darted out to lick the blood from the corner of his lips. Then he lazily toyed with the long braid running down Silver's back, waiting for her to finish saying whatever she needed.

This might not have ended this way if Shade hadn't been here to help. Colt was right, Sid needed to spend time at the Order and train. Now that he had different weapons at his fingertips, he would have to relearn how to fight.

Sid's bare feet crunched over rock and debris. He winced as sharp twigs stung. His adrenaline must have been too high to feel the pain before.

"Just kill them," Shade growled impatiently.

"No," Silver replied. "We have to give them a chance."

"Some of them already had a chance," Sid pointed out, nodding to the soldiers he'd faced and disarmed. Something familiar in their eyes halted him. Fear.

Sid was in their shoes once. He was who Shade had begged Silver to let him kill. But just like now, she'd stopped him. Even after that mercy, it had taken Sid months to change his mind about the Fae.

"But they need time," he added, agreeing with Silver. "Change doesn't happen overnight."

"If we see you back here," Shade snarled at them. "I'll be drinking my fill."

"Before we let them go," Sid said. "Let them see Nyra

and her mother bring this gully back to life. They need to witness it with their own eyes."

Nyra returned with her mother and a collection of bloody, vicious pixie soldiers still twitchy from battle. Moss and the dark-haired, blue-eyed soldier were there. They wanted to kill the prisoners, but Sid and Silver convinced them to wait.

Queen Juniper's expression was grave as she took her daughter's face in her hands. "You were right, Nyra. The Well had a purpose."

Her words came out breathless, as though she struggled to catch air. Her gaze skated to where Sid leaned against a tree, keeping a respectful distance. She beckoned him over. When he stood by Nyra's side and curled his arm around her shoulders, Juniper gave him a genuine smile.

"Your love for my daughter is bright in your eyes. You will be a good consort."

"Mother?" Nyra's voice turned tight. "What's wrong?"

"My darling daughter, it's time to pass you the reign." Juniper lifted the glass leaf tiara from her head and placed it on Nyra's head. She swallowed, and her sad eyes teared as she grasped her daughter's hands. "You are the new queen. The tithe belongs to you. The gully is yours to protect."

Unseen energy thickened the atmosphere. It was like lightning on Sid's tongue. A vibration. The gully taking a breath. Juniper slumped as Nyra gasped and lifted. Her back bowed as she floated, but her wings weren't holding her aloft. Worried, Sid reached for her, but Juniper's cool fingers wrapped around his wrist.

"She is receiving the tithe. Look how bright she glows... my daughter."

As though the sun powered Nyra's heart, a light glimmered from her pores and wings, spilling into the clearing. Everyone shielded their eyes until the light dimmed. When Sid looked back at his mate, she stood on the ground with a shocked expression and tears leaking. Wordlessly, she beckoned for Sid.

"Hurts," she choked out. "So much more than I ever felt. Mother was holding this pain for so long."

He clasped hands with Nyra, she closed her eyes, and Sid felt a pull through his equilibrium. Pain speared him, and he knew this must be the connection to the injured forest Nyra was talking about. That pulling feeling intensified, and strange things around the glade started happening. Lush ferns sprouted from the scorched earth. Metal bullets, weapons, trucks, barrows, the digger... it all sank like it was in quicksand. People hurriedly moved out of the way because Nyra's reparation to the land wasn't waiting. Life sprung anew in the gully. The pain in Sid's chest lessened. He could breathe again.

If only everyone could feel the pain when they hurt the world, perhaps they would take better care of it.

When it was done, when the forest was vibrant and green, Nyra opened her eyes and let go of Sid's hand. Unlike Juniper, who looked pale in comparison, Nyra's wings shone like diamonds. Her skin still glowed.

"Long live the queen," Juniper whispered, smiling as she lowered to her knees.

One by one, the pixie soldiers around Nyra dropped and announced their new loyalty. When Sid was the only one left standing, he looked to Silver and Shade but found them gone—and the surviving humans too. Shade must have taken them back to Crystal City.

His lips curved as he took his queen's hips in his hands. "You did it."

"We did it."

He lowered to his knees, still holding her thighs, and whispered, "Long live my queen. I will be with you every step of your reign."

"Promise?"

His heart clenched. This time when he answered, no hint of a lie was on his tongue. "Always. Forever."

FIFTEEN

"Y ou look incredible," Sid murmured as Nyra walked out of her dressing room in a floor-length ballgown.

It was made from a similar combination of gossamer, dainty leaves, and tiny white flowers as she'd worn on the day he met her. He couldn't stop staring. It reminded him too much of when he'd ripped that last dress to shreds. His throat went dry.

He dragged his gaze up to her smirking face and knew she was thinking the same thing. Her wings fluttered and she shivered. He might have glimpsed a glimmer of golden dust.

It was the night of the coronation ball. Even though Nyra had already been named queen, this celebration was supposed to happen on the day they'd met.

"You look rather dashing yourself, D'arn Sid." Nyra

sidled up to him and ran her fingers down the collar of his leather battle gear.

He'd received his Guardian uniform a week ago after meeting with the Prime. She was a hard, sometimes emotionless female, but she seemed like a good leader.

As the consort to a pixie queen, Sid still had a lot of education and training to complete. Her in the royal court and there at the Order. He had rules to adhere to, and missions that would take him away from Nyra, but it meant he could be proactive in his desire to atone for the wrongs he'd committed.

It bothered Sid that he wouldn't be here full-time to protect Nyra as the queen's consorts should, but Silver told him Shade never did as he was told. If Sid wanted to stay with Nyra, then he should.

"I feel weird," he admitted to Nyra. "Perhaps I should take off the uniform and wear something formal like the others."

"No," she gasped. "I like you in leather. Besides, it will do my subjects well to be reminded of your new job. That you're one of us. Not everyone will see the Guardian mark on your face, but they will see the uniform from any distance."

He glanced around their private royal suite. It existed inside another hollow of a tree, and now that Nyra had a greater capacity to hold mana, she could shift him to full size or small at any time. He felt a little out of place without wings, but he was finding his way about. As soon as he learned to control his own mana, he'd feel better.

He might even be able to borrow the ability to shift and grow his own wings. He tried not to keep his hopes up and hadn't told Nyra about the possibility yet.

Concern flickered in Nyra's eyes. "You're not still feeling like an outsider, are you?"

He gathered her into his arms and smiled gently down at her. "It's like you can read my mind."

His fingers must have clipped her wings because she shivered, her eyes darkened, and her voice became husky. "I know of another way to remind everyone you're one of us."

"What's that?"

Her wings vibrated, buzzed, and gold pixie dust glimmered along the membranes. As each particle landed on his skin, desire heated his blood.

"Fangs," he growled at her. "You know what this does to me."

"Yes." She gasped as he kissed her neck. "And if we arrive covered in dust, we will remind everyone that you're the only one who could make this happen."

She pulled him down to the plush bed covered in cushions. Then she pushed him onto his back. Seeing his mate come at him, all wicked intent, had his heart racing and his erection pulsing against its new leather confines.

Nyra hiked up her ballgown and then straddled him with a cheeky curve of her glossy lips. "Show me that smooth, gorgeous human dick."

"Fuck," he breathed, rocking into her as she untied his pants. He was so hard, it hurt. That he could go from nothing to aching in seconds, all because of her pixie dust, was magic.

She hadn't gone into heat since that first night, but she'd learned to create the dust with him whenever she wanted. With a greedy glint in her eyes, she freed his shaft and moaned as she pumped its length. Sid threw his head back and submitted to her.

"I'm going to make a mess," he growled.

"Then I'd better do something about that." She straddled his lap and guided his tip to her core, then lowered on his shaft until she was seated. They groaned as bliss filled them.

"So big," she praised.

Sid had to fist the sheets to stop himself from ruining the gown. Nyra took control. She used her wings to power each thrust of her hips, and he met her every time. The friction was delicious. Seeing the blush appear on her skin was the most satisfying sight. Gold dust kept falling, kept ratcheting their hunger and arousal until finally, Sid saw stars. Hot wave after wave of ecstasy burst through him. Nyra gave a strangled cry of passion, her thighs clenched, and she joined him in release.

"Oh my," she gasped as she fell on top of him afterward. "I think that gets better every time."

Still panting, although he didn't feel like he did much work, he held her hips with trembling fingers.

"Do you think we can ignore the ball and stay here?" he asked quietly, idly tracing his fingers along her arms as she lay on top of him.

She sighed. "I missed the first ball. I can't miss the second."

"You're right," he said, catching the blue glow of his new Guardian mark reflecting against her face. "We have all the time in the world to spend with each other."

Her violet eyes sparkled. "Promise?"

"I'll do you one better. I'll pinkie-promise." He held out his little finger but she smacked it away with a scowl.

"I think you mean pixie promise."

He laughed. "I love you. How's that?"

She softened against him. "Perfect. I love you too."

⚖

THANK you for reading Sid's and Nyra's story. It's a standalone novella in the Fae Guardians world, and there are already 9 full-sized novels before it where a growly and possessive fae protector falls in love with a woman—his human enemy.

Start with The Longing of Lone Wolves in Kindle Unlimited.

FIRST TIME IN ELPHYNE?

Check out the Fae Guardians from book one in Kindle Unlimited. You'll get plenty of growling protective fae mates, women who find their power within, angst, tension, and always spicy romance.

Season of the Wolf Trilogy

    1. The Longing of Lone Wolves

    2. The Solace of Sharp Claws

    2.5 Of Kisses & Wishes Novella (standalone novella)

    3. The Dreams of Broken Kings

Season of the Vampire Trilogy

    4. The Secrets in Shadow and Blood

    5. A Labyrinth of Fangs and Thorns

    6. A Symphony of Savage Hearts

Season of the Elf Trilogy

7. A Song of Sky and Sacrifice

7.5 Of Pixies and Promises (standalone novella)

8. A Crown of Cruel Lies

9. A War of Ruin and Reckoning

Why Choose Spin-Off

Fae Devils

Castle of Nevers and Nightmares

What's Next?

CAN'T WAIT THAT LONG FOR YOUR FAE GUARDIANS FIX?

Join Lana's VIP Angels in Patreon for exclusive bonus content, early access to ARCs and self-pubbed audiobooks, NSFW art, a monthly serial, and book box options.

Also by Lana Pecherczyk

THE FAE GUARDIANS WORLD

Fae Devils

(Fae Guardians Sluagh Spin-off)

Castle of Nevers and Nightmares

THE DEADLYVERSE

The Sinner Sisterhood

(Demon-hunting Paranormal Romance)

The Sinner and the Scholar

The Sinner and the Gunslinger

The Sinner and the Priest

The Deadly Seven

(Fated Mate Paranormal/Sci-Fi Romance)

The Deadly Seven Box Set Books 1-3

Sinner

Envy

Greed

Wrath

Sloth

Gluttony

Lust

Pride

Despair

ABOUT THE AUTHOR

Lana Pecherczyk is a neurodivergent paranormal and fantasy romance author from Australia. Two-time winner of the RWA Prism Award. She makes a mean chocolate cake and enjoys 'pro-caffeinating.' Basically, if it's got flawed, swoon-worthy men, strong women, spice, and page-turning action, then she'll write it because she loves to read it. She also wins love by daylight and fights evil by moonlight.

Subscribe.lanapecherczyk.com for free books
Join Lana's Faceboook Group to chat to other Readers
Check out more of Lana's books on Amazon

Printed in the USA
CPSIA information can be obtained
at www.ICGtesting.com
LVHW041438250124
769628LV00012B/524